Exotic I
Vol

By M.S. Parker

CW00504694

Copyright © 2015 Belmonte Publishing LLC
Published by Belmonte Publishing LLC.
ISBN-13: 978-1511736084

ISBN-10: 1511736089

Table of Contents

Chapter 1

Reed

Paris, France.

I'd arrived three days ago, coming by way of London, Glasgow, Vienna, and Rome, as well as Moscow and Berlin. None of these places were like home and I was grateful for that.

Home.

I ran my hand through my hair, ignoring the appreciative looks from the women in the café. I knew I was good-looking. I wasn't conceited, just honest. That was one of the vows I'd made to myself when I left Philadelphia a couple months ago. No more lies. Lies were the reason I'd been traveling around Europe, wearing out my welcome with various college friends. If I'd just been honest back then, with *her*, things might've turned out different.

I shook my head and drained the last of my drink. I didn't want to think about Piper Black. After all, the entire point of coming to Europe was to get away from her. I managed a wry smile. Another lie.

It wasn't just Piper I was running from, the same way it wasn't her who'd made me turn my entire life upside-down. She'd just been the catalyst who had started the whole damn thing.

I looked across the street to where the Eiffel Tower stood and took a moment to enjoy the regal landmark. I tossed a few bills onto the table and stood up. I hadn't been over to see it yet. I'd been a little more interested in the Paris nightlife than the city's history. After all, I was twenty-seven, far from an old man, and I'd spent the last five years of my life concerned more about work, about doing what my family expected of me. My little tour of Europe was my time to have fun.

I looked up at the tower and then around. After dismissing a few possibilities, I found exactly who I was looking for. Putting on my most charming smile, I approached her.

"*Bonjour. Voulez-vous me prendre en photo?*" I held up my phone.

"American?"

Her accent was thick, but I was more interested in how her long brown hair would look spread across my hotel bedspread or the way her curves would feel under my hands.

"Yes." I pulled my thoughts to the present. "I'm

Reed."

"Monique." She flashed teeth too straight to have been completely natural. The nose was a little too perfect too. My eyes flicked down to her ample breasts. Probably fake as well.

"Would you take my picture, Monique?"

"Of course." She took my phone, letting her fingers brush, then linger against mine.

I smiled at her as she snapped a shot of me with the tower in the background. When she handed me back the phone, I winked at her and, on a whim, sent the picture to Piper. I'd been keeping her updated on my trip. Well, more or less. Things hadn't exactly ended badly in the angry sense, just me being hurt. I wanted to let her know that I was okay. And I *was* okay...sort of.

"You are here alone?" Monique asked, her voice as erotic and soft as the finger she ran up my arm.

I was about to be very okay.

***

Monique's big brown eyes widened when she saw the hotel where I was staying, but she didn't seem overwhelmed. I'd definitely chosen well. I had no problem with Europeans who were enamored with Americans. What I didn't need was someone looking for money and a green card. Monique might not be Stirling rich, but she dressed well enough to let me know she wouldn't be coming after me for some big payday. There were too many women who thought they'd fuck me and I'd take care of them for life. Or the ones who tried to do things like get pregnant or some shit like that. Finding a random hook-up was getting to be as complicated as having a relationship.

Not that I'd really know. Pretty much all of my relationships had been shit.

"Reed?"

"Come on, *ma chérie*." I slid my arm around her waist and pulled her towards the elevator. "You're going to love the view."

As soon as the elevator doors closed, she was on me. Her mouth was firm, no hint of hesitation. Definitely something I liked about European women, especially the French. If they wanted someone, they went for it. I wrapped my arms around her waist and pulled her even more tightly against me. She moaned and nipped at my bottom lip. I dropped my hand lower and squeezed her ass. If she was half as good in bed as she was at kissing, this was going to be fun. And probably just what I needed.

The door to my room had barely shut behind us

4

and she was already unzipping her dress. I lost my shoes and started unbuttoning my shirt while I watched her slowly shimmy out of the confining material. I let out a low whistle. She looked even better out of the dress than she had in it.

"In case you are wondering." She ran her hands over her flat stomach and up to cup the crimson silk holding her breasts. "They are real."

Had I misjudged her? Could she really be this perfect?

She reached behind her and unhooked her bra, releasing a pair of the most magnificent breasts I'd ever seen. Easily a D-cup. She smiled at me as she hooked her thumbs in the waistband of her matching silk panties. She slowly lowered them, revealing something I'd come to learn about French women. They were as diverse as Americans when it came to their grooming habits.

"You like what you see?" she asked, running her fingers over her bare pussy.

I closed the distance between us in two quick steps and covered her mouth. My tongue pushed at her lips and they parted. I ran my hands over her back and down to that firm ass as I explored every crevice of her mouth. She tasted like coffee and expensive chocolate.

Her hands found their way under my shirt, palms burning against my skin. When her nails scraped over my nipples, I moaned and felt her smile. She broke the kiss and pushed my shirt from my shoulders.

"*Magnifique.*" She lowered her head and flicked her tongue against my nipple. She looked up at me through those thick eyelashes, gave me one of the most wicked grins I'd seen in a long time, and bit down.

"Shit!" I buried my hand in her hair as she worked her mouth across my chest, biting and licking until my cock was pressed painfully against my zipper. I'd barely spent a night alone since coming to Europe, but the last couple ones had been rather passive and I was starting to get bored. I'd definitely picked a good one today.

"Let us see what you have to offer." She went to her knees in front of me, her hands at my waist, making short work of my pants. Her dark eyes brightened as she lowered my pants and saw the bulge at the front of my underwear. "*Très bon.*"

"Like what you see?" I grinned down at her.

"Very much." She curled her fingers under the waistband of boxer-briefs and yanked them down.

My cock jutted out in front of me, thick and

hard, eager for attention. Monique reached around and grabbed my ass, nails digging into the muscle as she wrapped her lips around the head of my cock. I groaned as she circled the tip with her tongue, then took me deeper. Her mouth was wet and hot as she took me all the way to the root, her lips stretched wide around me.

"Fuck!" My hands curled into fists. Damn, she knew what she was doing.

One hand released my ass and came around to cup my balls. She rolled them as she bobbed her head, taking my cock all the way into her mouth and down her throat each time. A lot of women gave head because they thought it was expected or that it was the best way to get a man going. Then there were women like Monique, ones that obviously enjoyed it. Or were at least enthusiastic about it.

"*Ma chérie.*" My voice was strained. "That's enough."

The hand on my ass flexed, nails digging in, giving me a bite of pain to go with the pleasure. Then I was sliding from her mouth, my cock swollen and glistening. I held out my hand to her and she took it, letting me help her to her feet. It was then that I noticed she was still wearing her heels. Heels and nothing else. Fuck, that was hot.

7

She released my hand and gave me that naughty smile again. She licked her bottom lip, then bit her lip with those perfect teeth. She winked at me and sauntered over to the French doors. I kicked off my pants and underwear as I followed her, stopping only to grab a condom from my pants pocket. She pushed the curtains aside and put her hands on the glass. Feet apart, ass out. There was no doubt what she wanted.

I stood behind her, taking in the line of her body, the smooth skin of her back, the curve of her ass. She was gorgeous. Just like every other woman I'd fucked since coming to Europe. Sometimes I felt like that was the only thing I'd been doing. Party, drink, fuck. Repeat as needed. Hope that I'd somehow figure out what I was going to do. Where my life was supposed to go next. So far, it wasn't working.

Still, it didn't mean I would stop trying, especially with a woman who looked like this.

I ran my finger down her spine and she arched her back. I palmed her ass. Damn that was firm. My cock throbbed in anticipation, eager to finish what her mouth had started. It would have to wait though.

I leaned against her, pressing my cock against her leg. My hand dropped down between her legs.

"Already wet?" I dipped a finger inside her and she made a mewling sound. "Do you really like sucking dick that much?"

"Very much." She pushed back against my hand, but I didn't give her what she wanted.

"And what do you think I should do to you now?" I removed my hand and lightly smacked her ass. Based on what I'd seen, I thought she might like it and I wasn't proven wrong.

"Harder, *se il vous plaît*," she begged.

I brought my hand down a little more firmly and she let out a gasp that was pure pleasure. I alternated cheeks, each smack making her cry out. I didn't stop until my hand began to sting and her ass was a brilliant shade of red. I shook my hand as I bent down to pick up the condom I'd dropped. I tore it open and rolled the latex over my erection. The immediate need to come had eased a bit, but I was still ready to go.

I leaned my body over hers, intentionally rubbing against her sensitive ass as I did so. "I'm going to fuck you now." I cupped her breasts, squeezing them until she writhed against me. "Take you hard and fast right here against this window." I pinched her nipples and she made a sound half-way between a yelp and a moan. "Is that what you want?"

9

"Oui, se il vous plaît."

I didn't need to know French to understand that as a definite affirmative.

I kept one hand on a breast, pinching her nipple, as the other hand slid down her stomach and between her legs. She gasped as I found her clit and rubbed the tip of my finger across it. Just when I felt her body start to quiver, I stopped.

She let out a stream of French expletives that made me chuckle. I straightened and put one hand on her hip. I teased around her entrance with the tip of my cock until she shot a glare over her shoulder. With a snap of my hips, I drove myself into her and her glare turned into a beautiful portrait of overwhelming sensation. Her entire body jerked and she swore again. I stayed still, giving her a moment. There was a fine line between painful pleasure and straight pain. I liked the first, but never wanted to cause the latter.

I rolled my hips and she cried out. *"Prêt?"* I made sure to ask it in French so there'd be no misunderstanding. She seemed to like it rough, but I didn't want to start moving until I was sure she was ready.

She nodded her head and I pulled back until just the head was still inside her. When I thrust into her this time, she wailed loud enough for me to hope that no one was in the room next to mine...and that the glass door she leaned on would prevent the people outside from hearing her. Then again, if anyone looked up, there'd be no doubt as to what was happening.

She kept one hand on the glass and used the other to play with her nipples, pulling and twisting until they'd turned from pale pink to almost red. She pushed back against me with every stroke, forcing me deeper even as she squeezed my cock with her pussy.

"Fuck," I swore through gritted teeth. I didn't know where this girl had come from, but someone had definitely taught her how to fuck.

I moved my hand around to her front, once again finding her clit. She moaned as I rubbed the little bundle of nerves. The pressure inside me was building, but I was going to get her there first. I might not have always been the gentlest of lovers, but I liked to think of myself as considerate. I always did my best to make sure my partner came first.

"Spank me," she said, her voice as strained as I felt.

I smacked her ass twice and apparently that was all she needed. She came with a high-pitched squeal that would've made me wince if she hadn't clamped down on my cock at the same time and triggered my own orgasm. I closed my eyes as I came, focusing on the pleasure coursing through me, the way her muscles flexed around my cock, prolonging the pleasure until it almost hurt.

It was only during these moments that I felt at peace, that I forgot about all the shit I had waiting for me back in the States and the vast, empty future stretching out before me. A few precious moments where it was pure bliss and all was right in my world.

Then it was over.

Chapter 2

Reed

I'd always thought I had stamina, but Monique definitely put that to the test. By the time she left around midnight, I barely had enough energy to dry off from our joint shower and make it into bed before I fell asleep. The best part about being that exhausted was that I didn't dream.

I couldn't exactly say I'd been having nightmares before, because they weren't disturbing or anything like that. No, it was more like my brain had decided to deal with my issues when I was asleep since I refused do it when I was awake. Sometimes it was my parents asking me why I'd left and begging me to come home. The guilt trips my imaginary parents gave were almost as convincing as the real thing.

Then there were the ones with Piper.

Most of the time, my mind replayed every

moment we'd spent together, trying to figure out where things had gone wrong. What would've happened if I would've done things differently? Like if I'd told her the truth that day I'd run into her at my sister's high school reunion. Would we still have ended up in bed together or would she have turned me down when I'd kissed her that first time? What if I'd called my engagement to Britni off sooner? Would I still have ended up in Vegas, seeing Piper work, or would I have stayed in Philadelphia to look for her? What if I'd changed things later so that we'd still had the same meeting, but instead of being an ass and essentially asking her to be a bought-and-paid-for mistress, I'd broken up with Britni to be with Piper?

In some of the dreams, Piper and I ended up together in some sort of weird alternate universe where my family accepted her and my sister apologized for being a bitch for so many years. I always woke from those with my hand stretched out to the other side of the bed, thinking she would be there. Then I'd remember. Worse were the ones where, no matter what I did, she still ended up with *him*. In the dreams, I could feel how futile my attempts were, but couldn't stop myself from trying to make a difference. Either way, I'd wake up knowing that I'd lost her.

When she'd told me she didn't want us to be together, it cut me to the quick. She'd said that what we'd had hadn't been real. Maybe not for her, but I'd thought for sure it had been for me. Only over the past couple weeks did I start to wonder. I'd met her when I'd been very close to marrying a woman I didn't love, a woman my parents had decided was a good fit for me.

As much as it pained me, I couldn't help but wonder if I'd fallen for Piper because of timing and circumstances. I'd feelings for her, that much was true, and I'd wanted her – a man would have to be either gay or stupid not to want her – but was what I felt for her more than that?

I lay in bed, staring up at the ceiling. There was gratitude, I thought, for giving me a reason to divorce Britni. Or, more accurately, showing me the reasons to divorce my wife. That had started the chain reaction that had led me here. Part of my rationale for doing the things I'd done had been for Piper, but they'd also been for me. I'd spent so much of my life giving up things I wanted just to make my parents happy, to make my family proud, that I'd never considered what I wanted out of life. Until now.

I frowned. I'd spent the last couple months considering and wasn't any closer to an answer than I had been when I'd left Philadelphia.

My phone rang and I sighed, rolling over to grab it.

"Hello?"

"Good morning, Reed."

"Mom?" I blinked at the clock. She had to be up early to be calling me here. Then I registered the time. Almost noon. Which meant it was nearly seven o'clock back home.

"Are you just waking up?"

I flopped back on my pillows and closed my eyes. I was an adult, thousands of miles away, and she could still sound like I was some lazy kid sleeping in late.

"Yes, Mom, I am." There wasn't much point in lying to her.

"Your father's on the line too," she said.

Fuck. My parents had to be two of the few people who still had landlines and liked to use them for conference calls. I had a feeling if they'd been in charge of the technical advancements, our companies would still be using computers that took up a whole room.

"Morning, Dad," I said. I silently wondered what

16

the hotel would think if I threw my cell phone off the balcony and into the pool below.

"We need you to come home, Reed." At least Dad didn't try to make small talk. "You know I can't run the businesses by myself, not with my health."

Dad had been playing the health card since he'd been rushed to the ER three years ago with chest pains. The doctors had said it was a panic attack, but he'd refused to believe them, instead insisting that he'd had a heart attack and the hospital was conspiring against him. Conspiring with who and why, he never said. Only that there were people who wanted to make sure he was ruined. I was just grateful he kept his theories to himself. The last thing we needed was our stockholders thinking the old man was nuts.

"You have Rebecca to help you," I reminded him.

My little sister was in her early twenties and had been after my dad for the past couple years to let her run one of the companies. He'd always refused and I knew she thought it was because she was a girl. While that was part of it, I happened to know that my father also believed that Rebecca didn't have the temperament to be a good CEO. I didn't disagree.

"Rebecca doesn't know what she's doing," he

said bluntly.

"Your father and I tried to get her to see that," Mom cut in. "We even had things worked out with the Westmores to have Rebecca marry Blayne."

"Isn't he the screw-up?" I asked. From what I remembered, he was a couple years older than me, but was still acting like he was in high school. Maybe college if he was in a frat.

"His father had been eager to get his son married and settled. We thought he and Rebecca would be a perfect match."

Apparently, my parents hadn't learned from my disaster of a marriage that, in this day and age, in our culture, arranged marriages didn't work. Telling them that wouldn't do any good though so I kept my mouth shut and waited for them finish with their little pitch.

"Then he went out and married some immigrant or something."

I could almost see the condescending sneer on my mother's face. It was on the tip of my tongue to remind her that, while her family could trace its lineage back to the Mayflower, she was still descended from immigrants.

"Anyway." My father picked things back up. "After that incident, your sister decided she no longer wanted to listen to reason and was going to do things her own way."

I suppressed a laugh. I wasn't sure why that surprised them. Rebecca and I might've both been tall and had the same blond hair – hers dyed lighter while mine remained more golden – but that was where the similarities ended, physical and in personality. Her eyes were hazel while mine were a brown so dark they were almost black. I'd always toed the line while she hadn't cared what anyone said about her. The biggest difference was that I tried to be nice to people while Rebecca's idea of nice was a backhanded compliment and laughing behind someone's back.

"You worked so hard for that company, I can't understand how you can let her run it into the ground."

I sat up, my temper flaring at the attempt to manipulate me. "You guys used the company once to get me to marry Britni. I'm not letting you use it again. If Rebecca screws up, it's your own fault."

"You're the one who left, Reed." My father's voice was sharp. "You abandoned your family, neglected your responsibilities–"

"I'm going to stop you right there, Dad," I interrupted smoothly. "I've always done what you

19

expected of me. I went to Columbia and got an MBA because that's what you wanted. I went to work for the family business right after I graduated because that's what I was supposed to do. I married Britni. I almost had a kid with her."

"But you fucked that up, didn't you?"

"Lawrence!" My mom sounded shocked and I had to admit that I was a little surprised. My father rarely talked like that.

"I made a choice," I said quietly. "I chose me. I've had enough of doing everything I've been told to do. I'm not a child."

"Then you should stop behaving like one," Mom snapped.

"Figuring out what I want to do with my life is being a child?" I asked. "It's not like you support me. I have my inheritance, but I've also earned every penny of it as well as the salary I've received these past five years. I've never asked you for a dime. I'm an adult, and I deserve the opportunity to figure out what I want out of life."

"And what is that?" Dad asked. "Sleeping your way through half of Europe?"

"Nice to know you have people keeping tabs on me," I said. It didn't surprise me. I had a feeling the hotels where I'd stayed had been reporting my activities to my parents.

"Come home and take charge of the company again while you decide what you want to do," Mom suggested.

It was tempting, I thought. It was a solid job. I liked the people I worked with. But I knew if I went back, I'd never leave again. Breaking free the first time had been hard. Leaving a second time would be virtually impossible. I had to stay away.

"I don't think that's a good idea," I said. "I need to be away while I figure this out."

"This discussion isn't over," Dad said.

It was for me, but I didn't say that. They'd figure it out when nothing they said worked.

"I'll talk to you guys later then," I said.

"We love you, Reed," Mom said.

"Love you too." And it was true. I did love them. I just didn't want to be like them.

I ended the call and headed for the bathroom. First on the order of business for today was breakfast. After that, I planned to check out a few places I hadn't seen yet. I did appreciate good art and Paris was the perfect place to enjoy that. I was thinking two more weeks and then I'd be ready to move on again. I didn't want to overstay my welcome. I hadn't yet decided where I wanted to go, but wherever it was, it sure as hell wouldn't be Philadelphia. Not anytime soon.

Chapter 3

Nami

Paris, France.

I'd never been allowed to come here alone before. I threw a glance over my shoulder and scowled. I supposed I wasn't truly alone now either, but at least the two hulking masses behind me weren't my overprotective parents. When my parents had told me I would be allowed to take a trip across Europe after my college graduation, I'd been thrilled, sure that I had finally earned my freedom. After all, I had spent twenty-two years being the dutiful daughter. I did as I was told, everything from what classes to take, to who my roommate was allowed to be. I had been a good girl and stayed in my room studying while others went to parties, flirted and drank. I had disobeyed only once and my parents didn't know about the night I'd snuck out to see my friend, Aaron.

23

I sighed as I thought of him. Aaron Jacobs. He'd been a friend since freshman year. Sweet, kind. The kind of man a normal girl would've been thrilled to take home to her parents. I hadn't allowed myself to become attached because I'd known that it would never work between the two of us. I'd been honest with him upfront, and he, in turn, had been honest with me. We'd become close friends, and my parents had been nervous until I introduced them to Aaron's boyfriend.

Well, I supposed there was that one little thing that would've given some parents pause. Aaron was bisexual. I hadn't told my parents that though. Not because they would have freaked out about him being attracted to men, but because being bisexual would've meant he could've still wanted me. No, I'd simply made sure he had his current boyfriend present the first time I introduced him to my parents and they'd never worried about him after that.

I smiled to myself. They should have. I'd made it clear to Aaron from moment one that we couldn't have a relationship, but as graduation had approached four years later, I'd asked him for a favor. He'd been single at the time and I'd been adamant that I wasn't going to go home a virgin. My bodyguards had gotten a bit lax those last couple weeks, prompted, I supposed, by the previous four years of good behavior. Whatever the reason, I'd been able to get to Aaron's dorm, do the deed, and get back before my guards realized I was gone.

I didn't regret it, especially now. I scowled at my reflection, hating the face that looked back at me. I had my father's chin and nose, my mother's cyan eyes and figure. The dark brown curls and tanned skin were the result of combining my mom's fair coloring with my father's darker coloring. I'd been told more than once that, had I not been barely five feet tall and on the curvy side, I could've been a model. The exotic look was all the rage.

I almost wished I had been tall enough. I could only imagine the look on my father's face if I had told him I planned to be a model. My parents weren't completely old-fashioned, but there were certain areas where tradition still held a high bar, and my sex life was one of those areas.

I'd said that Aaron would've been the kind of boy a normal girl could've taken home to her family. The problem was that I wasn't a normal girl. I was Princess Nami Carr, eldest child of King Raj and Queen Mara. My family had ruled the tiny island nation of Saja for thousands of years. No one had really ever heard of Saja. We pretty much kept to ourselves, didn't bother with world politics or anything like that. We didn't crave the spotlight or had any important natural resources to exploit. We had nice beaches and pretty waterfalls, but we didn't sell ourselves as a tourist trap. We were fairly self-sufficient and liked it that way.

I loved my home, and my family. I just didn't love being a princess. I knew there were millions of girls who'd kill to be in my shoes, but they didn't get it. I wasn't just another princess. I was the crown princess, which meant I was destined to rule one day. And that meant there were certain things I didn't get to do.

Like choose a career.

Fall in love.

Choose whom I would marry.

Which is what brought me back to my current situation. My parents' graduation gift had actually been more of a bribe, or at least a way to put me in a better mood for when they dropped that particular bombshell on me.

Once I returned from Europe, I would be marrying a man they had already chosen. There would be an official engagement announcement, of course, and some sort of party for us, but the betrothal was set and the wedding would follow shortly. Most likely within a couple months of my arrival. Everything but the dresses, color scheme and flowers will have already been planned by the time I arrived home. As the princess, those were the only things I had a say in. My attendants would be picked for me, members of other noble families who my parents needed to keep happy. The only one I could count on would be my maid of honor, my sixteen year-old sister, Halea.

The guest list would be carefully selected and pruned until every seat was filled and no one important was offended. The location would be the palace, naturally. Saja was a nation of myriad religions and my parents wouldn't want to insult any of them by seeming to favor a specific location or have one religion oversee the officiating. That would be my father's job. As king, he would conduct the ceremony to ensure that no one religion was shown preferential treatment.

The finest dressmakers in Saja would be on call when I returned to do any necessary alterations to whichever dress I picked. That selection would come from a small number of appropriate dresses chosen by my mother. The same would go for my bridesmaid's dresses and the flowers.

As for my future husband, I knew nothing about him. My parents had said only that he would be handsome and from a good family. That was what mattered to them. To his family, I knew what they would care about. Saja's ruling line was very clear. Eldest child to eldest child, regardless of gender. Ironically, I would one day govern the entire island, but until my father passed, I had no say in my own life. While my husband would be king in name, I would be the ruler. But, once I had his child, his family's bloodlines would be forever linked to the throne. That was why my virginity was so important. The family would want assurances that it was their son's child I bore and no one else's. His virginity and fidelity didn't matter to them. Even as king, no bastard of his would have a right to the throne. He could have as many of those as he wanted.

Maintaining my purity was the main reason Thug One and Thug Two – otherwise known as Tomas and Kai – had been assigned to me the moment I'd left Saja. On the island, everyone knew who I was and no one would dare put themselves in a situation where anything improper could even be insinuated. A lot of girls assumed that being a princess meant always having dates to events like dances and proms. Not for me. What guy was brave enough to approach a girl flanked by security and ask her to go out with him? The answer was none.

I'd graduated from Princeton with a degree in political science – my parents' choice – and a minor in classical literature – my choice – but had nothing else to show for my four years in America. No friends aside from Aaron, and I knew I'd never see him again. No adventures or whirlwind romances. I couldn't even claim to have had four years where I didn't have to think about my responsibilities. I'd hoped this trip would be that opportunity for me, even if just for a couple weeks. Instead, it was just another reminder of what was expected of me.

"Princess, are you ready?" Kai spoke from his position at the door. His accent was rougher than mine, denoting the part of Saja he was from. "Your dinner reservations are in thirty minutes."

Of course they were. I had a schedule to keep. Appearances to make. My parents had managed to turn my graduation present into a royal event as well. I was expected to be seen in all the right places. I'd gone straight to London after graduation and stayed there for three days. Now, it was a few days in Paris and then on to Italy where I'd have a couple days before going home. Today was my last day in Paris and I'd been to several museums, five-star restaurants and taken in some of the sights. And I'd been bored out of my mind. I supposed I wouldn't have minded as much if I'd had someone to enjoy things with, but my bodyguards were strictly professional. They spoke only when spoken to; offered no opinions save ones that had been given to them by the king. And, most importantly, made sure I behaved.

I turned away from the mirror. "No, Kai. I'm actually not feeling well. I think I'll spend the rest of the night in bed."

"Do you need for us to call a doctor?" he asked.

I shook my head. "I'll be fine." I walked back into my bedroom and closed the door. I looked in the full-length mirror. I'd dressed the way I was expected to dress for a dinner out. My parents may have made a big deal about my virginity and modesty in dress, but they both understood fashion. The pantsuit I wore had been designed specifically for me for this trip and I looked poised, elegant, and like I was about to walk into a courtroom or board room. All business.

I wanted fun.

I stripped off the clothes and hung them over the desk chair. My heart was pounding as I picked up the bag I'd carefully hidden from my bodyguards.

We'd gone shopping earlier today and I'd purchased several outfits of clothing appropriate for a princess...and one dress I knew my parents would have instantly vetoed. Tomas and Kai hadn't seen it because I hadn't modeled any of the clothes, but I'd had to give the saleswoman cash and ask her to ring the dress up separately, putting it in a small bag inside the other bag.

I opened the bag now and pulled out my small act of rebellion. I slipped it on and looked at myself again. Now I looked like a twenty-two year-old college graduate ready to enjoy Paris. It was a deep shade of blue that made my eyes stand out and flattered my curves. The hemline hit me mid-thigh, still modest but far shorter than anything my parents would've let me wear. The neckline was plunging, nearly revealing my bra, but still covered more than some of the things I'd seen the women here wearing.

I pushed my hair back from my face, tousling the curls into their usual haphazard mess. I'd cut it short my first day in London, butchering it purposefully so I'd have no other option than to go to a stylist and let her trim it even shorter. Tomas and Kai hadn't been happy about that and I knew they were dreading my parents' reaction. I didn't care. I was tired of being good and I knew that I had a lifetime of decisions being made for me or decisions made based on what was best for my people. For this short bit of time, I wanted to do things my way.

I glanced towards the balcony. So far, my rebellion had been little things. My hair would grow again. No one had to see the dress. Now, however, was the defining moment and I had the feeling that if I went through with it, things were going to change.

I walked over to the doors and opened them, stepping out onto the balcony. I was on the fourth floor, which meant it was too far for me to risk jumping, but I'd come up with a plan yesterday when I'd first started batting this idea around. When the family traveled, we always bought out the rooms on either side of where we stayed to ensure extra privacy. My parents had done the same thing when they'd made my reservations. The room on the right had a balcony too, only a couple feet away from mine. I'd slipped the maid some money this morning to make sure the doors to the balcony were unlocked. Even in this dress, I wouldn't have a difficult time getting to that balcony. Once there, I'd go through the room, into the hallway and off to freedom.

For a few hours anyway.

Chapter 4

Nami

I couldn't believe that it actually worked. Getting across to the balcony had taken some balance, but it had been easier than I'd hoped. The maid had left the door unlocked and neither Tomas nor Kai had come out into the hallway when I'd slipped out of the room. I made it down to the lobby without anyone seeing me and then gave the desk clerk a little nod and a wave like I wasn't doing something wrong. Even if he thought to call up to the room, it wouldn't do any good. I'd left the hotel phone off the hook.

I caught a cab without any problem and was then on my way. Free, for a few hours at least.

It was too early for the best clubs to be open, but I didn't care. I'd get there eventually. I was a bit overdressed for regular sight-seeing, but I ignored the funny looks I got when I walked into the bookstore I'd spotted yesterday. It, of course, hadn't been on the list of approved stores for me to visit, but now I could spend all the time I wanted browsing the titles. No one there cared how I was dressed.

It was nearing eight by the time I made it to a restaurant to eat, and I purposefully chose one that wasn't five stars. The food was great and the atmosphere noisy. I loved it. I relaxed in my corner table, enjoying my food, and watching the people. Like most of the people on Saja, I spoke my own native dialect as well as English. I'd also been taught French, Russian, Spanish and some basic Chinese and German. I had a bit of Italian too, but not much. That was one of the things my parents had mentioned I'd be learning when I got back. We might not have had much interaction with other countries, but we were always prepared. Most of the people in the restaurant spoke English or French, so I listened to snippets of conversation, appreciating the banality of it all. Ordinary lives fascinated me.

When I left the restaurant, I finally headed to a club. The driver assured me that this was the hottest place in the entire city, if I could get in. That wasn't a problem. I was fully prepared to flash my passport since it contained my royalty status, but I ended up not needing it. The man working the door immediately waved me through and I stepped into the pulsing chaos.

It took a moment for my eyes and ears to adjust to the lights and the music, but as soon as they did, I was in heaven. No one here was whispering about me. Looks were either admiring or dismissive. A bit of jealousy from a couple women, but I knew it was based on appearance only, nothing more. No one here knew who I was.

At college, I'd wanted to keep a low profile, and since there were a lot of other people from prestigious or famous families, I'd thought it would be possible. Then, during freshman orientation, a cute guy had decided to sit next to me and strike up a conversation. Tomas and Kai had put a stop to that, announcing to the entire group that I was a princess and off limits. After that, Aaron had been the only one with enough guts to talk to me. Even the girls who would've normally tried to suck up to me kept their distance.

I wove my way through the crowd, heading for the bar. I had no intention of getting drunk, but I was strung tight and needed something to take the edge off. Ditching Tomas and Kai had been bad enough, but being here would piss my parents off to no end if they found out. I also had absolutely no clue how to behave. This was so far out of my element that, for a moment, I considered leaving, sneaking back into my room and curling up in bed like I'd told Tomas and Kai I'd intended to do.

"Bonjour, belle. Puis-je vous offrir un verre?"

A deep voice came from behind me and I turned towards it. His French was flawless, but I detected the American accent that marked him as not being a native.

"I already have a drink, but thank you." The words were out of my mouth before I stopped turning and I immediately regretted them as I found myself staring at one of the most gorgeous men I'd ever seen. Messy golden blond hair, eyes that looked black under the club lights. He was tall, easily over six feet, and lean, but not skinny. Features that were just a hint too masculine to be pretty, but close. Full lips that curved into an easy smile.

"You're not French," he said, leaning closer so he didn't have to speak so loudly.

I shook my head, but didn't expound.

"You don't sound American either," he said. His eyes narrowed like he was studying me, trying to puzzle me out.

"I'm not," I said. "Are those my only two options?"

His smile widened. "Reed Stirling."

"Nami Carr." I found myself returning the smile. There was something about him that appealed to me, and it wasn't just his looks.

When I'd first met Aaron, there had been this kind of click between us. I'd never experienced it with anyone before or since, until now.

"Let's dance."

Reed grabbed my hand and I gasped as a shock ran all the way up my arm. Based on the look of surprise on Reed's face, he'd felt it too. I could've written it off as some sort of static shock, the kind a person got when they touched metal, but I didn't think that was very accurate. Heat burned its way across my skin from the point where our hands touched and I knew I was blushing. I never blushed.

He pulled me towards him as we reached the dance floor and then released my hand. I had a moment to be disappointed and then he was moving to the music. He had the sort of feline grace that sometimes came with someone of his build and I wondered how that translated into the bedroom. My blush turned to flame and I silently scolded myself as I started to sway in time with the music. I'd come here to let loose a bit, not hook up with some random American, no matter how hot he was.

Then he put his hand on my waist and it was like I could feel every cell in my body waking up. His fingers curled possessively around me, pulling me closer to him so that our bodies brushed together as we danced. The music thrummed around us, but despite the sea of people, my world narrowed down to just him and me. His eyes locked with mine, pools of warm darkness, and I couldn't look away. My pulse pounded against my chest, my heart in my throat. I'd never been as aware of someone as I was of him right now.

Without consciously thinking about it, I raised my hand and pushed his hair away from his eyes, the strands damp with sweat. My fingers traced down his cheek and I felt the muscles in his jaw tense. The hand on my waist slid around to my back and he drew me against him until there was nothing between us but our clothes. I felt the swell of him against my stomach and it sent a thrill through me.

Sex with Aaron had been good. He was attractive and had been the kind of lover that most women would want for their first time. He'd made sure I'd climaxed before him and I'd thoroughly enjoyed myself. Afterwards though, I hadn't really had a desire for a repeat performance. In fact, sex hadn't really been something I'd thought much about. If my parents hadn't made such a big deal about me not doing it, I probably wouldn't have even slept with Aaron.

Now, with Reed's body flush against mine, his

desire for me clear, I wanted it. I wanted him. Aaron had appreciated my body and he'd genuinely cared about me, but he hadn't wanted me. Not really. Not at a primal level. Reed did. I saw it on his face and my body responded. I knew it was a bad idea. A terrible idea, actually, but I'd never wanted anything as badly as I wanted him right now.

I was teetering on the edge of decision as we continued to move to the music. It didn't have to be anything more than a hook-up. For all I knew, that's all Reed wanted too. I wasn't looking for a relationship. I couldn't. But sex, no matter how many times people said it didn't, always came with strings attached. Both sides had to know what was expected or feelings would be hurt, accusations made. When I'd gone to Aaron to ask him to be my first, I'd laid it all out for him. What it would mean for us, for our friendship. What it couldn't be. I'd known him and trusted him. I didn't know Reed.

Would it be possible for me to have that same conversation with him? Tell him that all I could offer him was one night? Most men wouldn't have a problem with that, I assumed. Especially an American man in a Parisian club. This wasn't exactly the kind of place someone went to find a soulmate.

There was also the safety factor to consider. I

didn't want to even think about it, but I had no way of knowing the kind of man Reed was. I could feel how strong he was, see it in the way he moved. If he wanted to hurt me, he could. I knew a little self-defense, but I'd never really needed to think about it. I'd always had bodyguards to protect me.

I couldn't do it. It would be reckless, irresponsible, dangerous, and a lot of other adjectives I knew my parents would've used.

Even as I opened my mouth to excuse myself before I got caught up in the moment, movement at the corner of my eye caught my attention.

Shit.

They'd found me.

Chapter 5

Reed

I'd fully expected to spend most of my night trying to decide who I wanted to take back to my hotel room, but I'd only been at the club for a few minutes when I saw her. She was beautiful, and not in a stick-figure model kind of way. No, she was all woman. Short, but not petite. Exotic coloring and the sort of confidence that could be spotted across the room. Without hearing her say a word, I could tell this woman was used to holding her own against anyone. Even better, she had a quick wit and the intelligence in her eyes was a welcome difference from most of the women I'd been sleeping with recently.

She wasn't French or American, I realized after she spoke. Her English was flawless, but there was a hint of an accent I couldn't quite place. That was okay though. I only cared what it would sound like when she was moaning my name. When we began to dance, I became more certain that I had to have her. She moved perfectly with me, the kind of instant synchronization that rarely happened and I knew it would transfer to how we'd move together in a far more intimate setting.

I was getting ready to ask her if she wanted to get out of here when she suddenly stiffened. I frowned, following her gaze. Did she have a boyfriend or husband who was going to come after me? Then I saw two absolutely massive men scanning the crowd.

Shit. Who was this girl?

I looked down at her. Myriad emotions ran across her face before she settled on something I recognized quite well: rebellious determination. She grabbed my hand and pulled me after her deeper into the dancing throng. I followed, too surprised by the gesture and how strong she was to argue about it.

We went out the back entrance and found ourselves in an alley that smelled a lot less pleasant than the club had. She made a face, but didn't stop until we stood on the sidewalk behind the club.

"Did you drive here?" she asked. "Rental car?"

I shook my head. "Taxi."

She looked up and down the street and then up at me. "Do you have a hotel room or are you staying with friends?"

I doubted I was misreading the signals, but I asked just to be sure. "I have a room. Would you like to go back there with me?"

She took a step towards me and wrapped her arms around my neck, pulling my head down even as she pushed herself up on her tiptoes. I slid my arms around her waist as her mouth met mine. Her lips were soft and pliant, molding around mine. As I traced her bottom lip with the tip of my tongue, her mouth opened eagerly and her tongue came out to meet mine. The two twisted together for a moment and then she was stepping back.

"This can only be tonight," she said. "I need that to be clear."

I grinned. A woman after my own heart. "Sounds good to me." I stretched out my arm and waved down a taxi.

"Where are you staying?" she asked suddenly, as if something had just occurred to her.

"Hôtel Maison Souquet."

A relieved look crossed her face.

"I'm guessing that's not where you are?"

She shook her head. "Hôtel San Régis."

My eyebrows went up. I'd known she'd had money just by the way she was dressed, but that was definitely one of the swankier hotels in Paris. It was also one that boasted discretion, more out of the way. People who went to clubs like the one Nami and I had just been at usually didn't stay at places like the San Régis.

She'd tensed again and watched me warily. For the first time, I realized that I wasn't sure what I'd gotten myself into. Huge guys like the ones back at the club didn't come looking for random girls. They were security somewhere or, if she was telling the truth about where she was staying, for someone. I smiled to put her at ease, but I kept watching her, trying to figure out if I'd seen her somewhere before. She was too short to be a model and too curvy, but she could've been an actress. Musician. And there was always the rich family option. As we pulled up in front of the hotel, however, I decided it didn't matter. Like she'd said, it wasn't like we were planning on starting a relationship. As long as she wasn't married, I didn't care about who she was.

As I held out my hand to help her from the car, I discreetly checked out her left hand. No ring, no tan line or faint impression. I supposed she could've taken it off or not have worn it long enough to leave any other mark behind, but short of ruining the mood by straight up asking her, it was all I had to go by.

I kept a grip on her hand as we walked through the lobby to the elevators. She didn't seem impressed by the opulence, lending further credence to my theory that she came from money. When we stepped into the elevator, I pushed all of that aside and concentrated on the only thing that mattered.

I backed her against the wall and claimed her mouth again, exploring it thoroughly. She made a little sound in the back of her throat that went straight to my cock. I grasped her wrists in my hands, pinning them against the wall as I ground my hips against her. The sound turned into a moan. Oh, she was going to be fun.

Before the door of my hotel room closed, we were kissing again, pulling at each other's clothes. I could feel the desperation in her touch and it fueled my own desire. By the time we reached the bedroom, we were both naked, our clothes leaving a trail behind us. It wasn't until we fell back on the bed that I finally moved my mouth from hers.

I leaned on my elbow as I began to kiss my way down her body, my free hand exploring her soft skin as well. She cried out as I flicked my tongue across her nipple, then made a louder sound when my fingers began to tease the other one. Her breasts were amazing. Firm, perfectly shaped and just the right size. Her nipples were a dusky rose color and, if her reaction was any indication, extremely sensitive.

I took one between my lips, looking up at her while I did it. Her eyes were closed and an expression of pure bliss had settled on her face. Damn. Either this woman loved sex or her previous lovers hadn't taken care of her nearly as well as they should've. I scraped my teeth across the tip of her nipple and her entire body jerked, her eyes flying open.

I raised my head. I may have liked things a little rough, but I wasn't about to assume that she did too. "Was that okay?"

"Do it again." Her pupils were wide, the thin ring of color around them dark.

I repeated what I'd done, a little harder this time, and she watched. Air hissed from between her teeth.

"Yes." She dropped her head back down onto the bed.

I took that as an affirmative and resumed what I'd been doing. She writhed underneath me as I began to suck on her hardening nipple. The sounds that she made were like nothing I'd ever heard before. Half whimpers, half moans and, mixed in were words in a language I didn't know. I couldn't wait to hear what she did when I was buried inside her.

Reluctantly, I left her breast and moved further down her body. If I'd had more time, I would've loved to see if I could get her to come just from that alone, but I didn't know how long she planned to stay. As I settled between her legs, I looked up and saw her watching me again, something on her face that it took me a moment to place. Uncertainty.

"Do you want to stop?" I hoped to hell she said no because my cock was almost painfully hard, but I'd never forced a woman and I never intended to. For a brief moment, I remembered how I'd felt when I'd learned about my former brother-in-law nearly raping Piper and my stomach knotted.

"No."

Nami's voice brought me out of the past and back to the present.

"Please don't stop."

I kissed the inside of her thigh. "I won't until you come."

Desire flared in her eyes and then I turned my

attention to what was right in front of me. She was already wet and I felt a surge of pride that I'd turned her on that much just from the little we'd done. When my tongue flicked out to taste her, she gasped. I used my fingers to hold her open, exposing as much of her as possible to my tongue. She cried out, her hands grasping the bedspread as I teased her clit.

I covered every inch of her, exploring this part of her body as thoroughly as I'd done her mouth previously. I felt her starting to tense and rubbed the flat of my tongue across her swollen clit, coaxing her towards the release I knew she had building. Suddenly, it hit her and her body stiffened. She made a muffled sound and I looked up to see her hand in her mouth, as if she couldn't bring herself to let it all go.

I was determined to see her lose control the next time she came. I wanted to hear her scream my name.

As she was coming down, I slid a finger inside her. Her pussy gripped it tight, still quivering from her orgasm. Damn she was tight. I looked up at her, hoping she'd answer my question in the negative.

"Are you a virgin?"

She gave me a smile that was half coy, half shy.

"No. But I'm not very...experienced."

I nodded. I could work with that. I moved my finger slowly, letting her body adjust to the intrusion before adding a second one. She moaned as I stretched her, preparing her. I put my hand on her stomach, just below her bellybutton, holding her against the bed as I crooked my fingers, searching for that special spot inside her. A sound half like a squeal, and half like a wail came out as I found it. I pressed my fingertips against the spot, rubbing it until she came again. She tightened around me until I swore. I kissed her inner thigh, waiting for her to relax again.

As she began to come down, I slid my fingers out and went up onto my knees. I leaned over her, reached into the bedside table and pulled out a condom. By the time I'd opened it and rolled it on, Nami was staring up at me, pure desire written on her face. I put my hands on her knees and started to slowly slide them up her legs.

"There are so many ways I want to take you," I said as my fingertips teased along her thighs. "So many things I want to do to you."

Something flitted across her face, some kind of regret and I knew that we didn't have the time. Whatever was going on with this young woman, her decision to leave with me had been impulsive.

I leaned over her, capturing her mouth again as I entered her. I groaned at the sheer heat of her and she responded by sucking my bottom lip into her mouth. Her body trembled beneath mine as I slowly slid into her and it took all of self-control not to bury myself into her with one thrust.

She wrapped her legs around me, pulling me in fast and hard. She cried out as I reached the end of her. Her body tightened and I pressed my face against the side of her neck. Every cell in my body screamed at me to move, to finish it, but I fought it back, wanting to enjoy this as much as possible. We fit together so well and her responsiveness was like nothing I'd experienced before. I couldn't wait to see what she did when I started to move inside her.

When I was sure I could move without embarrassing myself, I pulled back a bit and then surged forward. She cried out, her back arching up.

"Too much?" I asked. I could hear the strain in my voice.

She shook her head. "Please don't stop." Her accent had thickened.

I didn't hesitate, every nerve thrumming. I began to move, driving into her deep and hard. Her nails dug into my forearms as her body moved against mine.

"Fuck," I growled. If she wasn't experienced, how the hell did she know how to move like that?

I wrapped my arms around her, pulling her up onto my lap as I rocked back on my knees. I buried my hand in her hair, yanking her head to the side. She raked her nails down my back and I hissed as pinpricks of pain intensified the pleasure I was feeling. I scraped my teeth across her neck.

"No marks," she gasped.

I nodded and used her hair to bend her back. I freed a hand to grasp her breast, lifting it until my mouth closed around her nipple. I felt her still holding back even as our bodies moved together. I took a hard pull on the sensitive flesh and earned a bit of a whimper. Not good enough. She was close. I could feel it. I was too. I needed her to come, and I wanted her to come hard.

I bit down on her nipple, hard enough to hurt, but not to mark. The sound she made wasn't quite a scream, but it was close and all I needed. As her body shook around mine, I found my release. I held her tight, riding out our pleasure until we were both coming down.

Even as the sensations faded, I knew the awkward moment was coming. The decision of how long to let her stay, of what to say. But right now, it was still just us, just two people enjoying each other's bodies. I ran my hand down her spine. Maybe I could convince her to wait for another go around. I wanted to see her on top of me, those beautiful breasts bouncing...

My post-orgasmic brain was still hazy as it began to run through scenarios, but it cleared almost instantly when I heard someone calling out in the main room.

"Mr. Stirling, I'm so sorry, they just..."

Too many things happened at once.

The manager's voice trailed off as the bedroom door banged open.

Nami pulled away from me, rolling onto the bed and grabbing the bedspread as she went.

I turned towards the door to see two enormous men coming at me.

"Stop!" Nami shouted from behind me. She then rattled something off in what I assumed was her native language.

The men both froze, equally horrified expressions on their faces. Whatever Nami was saying to them, they didn't like it. What I didn't like was the way they were looking at me.

Who the hell was this girl?

Chapter 6

Nami

My hands were shaking so badly that I almost couldn't hold the blanket up high enough to cover my breasts. I hadn't expected Tomas and Kai to find me so fast. I certainly hadn't expected them to come busting in to Reed's hotel room.

Of course, their initial thought had been that he'd kidnapped me and was forcing me to have sex with him. I knew they'd think that from the moment I heard the manager yell from the main room. They'd stopped because I'd told them to, then they'd frozen because I'd informed them that I wasn't a virgin anymore.

Reed was looking back and forth between me and the men, completely baffled. I felt bad for him, but now wasn't the moment to explain. With as much authority as I could muster while sitting in a bed naked except for the hotel's bedspread, I quickly informed Tomas and Kai that should they deem it necessary to tell my father or mother about this, I would feel obligated to tell my parents that I had, in fact, actually lost my virginity back at Princeton while they were supposed to have been watching me. I saw the realization on their faces, the knowledge that no matter what they said, they were the ones who'd be screwed if this came out.

"Leave." I switched back to English for Reed's sake. Neither man moved, their eyes darting towards Reed and then back to me. "He's already seen me naked," I snapped. "You two don't get to. Out! Now!"

Their faces matching shades of red, they left, Tomas slamming the door behind him.

"Um, Nami?" Reed turned to look at me, his eyes wide. "What the hell was that about?"

"I am sorry, Reed," I said, climbing out from under the covers. I grabbed for my clothes, unable to look at him. "I wish things could be different. I wish I could spend tonight in this room with you."

I swallowed hard, myriad emotions choking me. I wished I could tell him all the other things I wanted. To be able to choose my own path, my own life. I couldn't say any of that though.

"I have to go. I have a train to catch in the

morning." I fixed my dress and allowed myself a glance at Reed. He was watching me with those dark eyes, an unreadable expression in them. "I'm sorry."

I walked out without another look back. Tomas and Eli were waiting just a couple feet away from the door, their faces back in those expressionless masks they always wore. I didn't have to see what they were thinking to know it. They thought less of me for what I'd done. I kept my head up though. I had nothing to be ashamed of. A woman taking charge of her sex life wasn't something bad or wrong, and I wouldn't let them make me feel bad about it.

"How did you find me?" I asked as we stepped into the hallway. I held up a hand before either of them could speak. "Never mind. I don't care."

"Your father called," Tomas spoke.

I was always surprised at Tomas's voice. He didn't talk much, especially to me, but when he did, it always made me want to laugh because it was so soft and almost feminine. At the moment, however, nothing was funny.

"He did?" I tensed as we stopped at the elevator.

"Mr. Mikkels has been monitoring the media."

"Of course he has," I muttered. Mikkels was my father's PR person. He'd been adamantly against me going to Princeton, sure that I'd be a public relations nightmare. Even after four years of model behavior, he didn't like me. He'd hated the idea of me going on a trip to Europe, making it clear that he thought I'd go wild the moment I stepped foot in London. To my credit, I had at least waited a while before I ran off to a club.

"It seems that there was a model at the club and you were in one of the pictures a reporter took," Kai said.

Shit. That couldn't lead to anything good.

"Your father has decided that it is time for you to come home," Tomas said.

"I have a week of my trip left," I said, walking out of the elevator ahead of the men.

"King Raj was quite insistent that we take you to your train first thing in the morning. Once we arrive in Italy, we're to make sure you are on the plane immediately."

"Dammit," I muttered under my breath. Apparently me telling Reed I had a train to catch wasn't a lie after all. I caught Kai giving me a disapproving look at my use of language. "Do you have a problem?" I snapped at him.

"No, Princess," he replied stiffly.

I would've felt bad for getting smart with him if I hadn't been fuming about my father's orders. Tomas and Kai had been stuck with me for over four years, away from home and everyone they knew. Neither of them were married or had kids, but I knew that Tomas had a large extended family, including several nieces and nephews, and Kai's mother was elderly and sick. I suspected he'd taken the job to pay for quality care for her. Saja had only two nursing homes on the entire island and it wasn't easy getting someone in there.

A limo was waiting for me in front of the hotel. Kai climbed into the passenger's seat while Tomas followed me into the back. The best thing about my bodyguards was that neither of them ever tried to strike up a conversation. That could be a bad thing if I wanted a distraction from the chaos in my head, but right now, I appreciated being able to think uninterrupted.

Well, not think so much as daydream. I didn't want to think about the future and what would happen when I got home. Right now, I wanted to enjoy the memory of my last vestiges of freedom.

While I'd had fun at the club, it hadn't been until Reed had approached me that I'd truly begun to enjoy myself. It had been crowded and loud, with people pressing all against me. I hadn't realized how much I'd gotten used to the little bubble of personal space that who I was had always accorded. Even at school, people hadn't tried to get close since Tomas and Kai had always been there, lurking in the background.

I wondered if Reed would've tried to talk to me even if Tomas and Kai had been there. Remembering the way he'd carried himself, the self-assured way he'd spoken, I thought he would have. He didn't seem like the kind of man who was intimidated by anyone.

I clasped my hands together on my lap, resisting the urge to run them over my neck, across my body, following the path his hands had taken. I could almost feel them, hot against my skin. The nipple he'd bitten throbbed, every movement chafing even as it sent a thrill through me. Aaron had been a good lover, at least I'd assumed so. He hadn't hurt me and I'd come with him, but it had been purely physical pleasure. There had been none of the fire I'd felt with Reed. When he'd been inside me, I'd felt like I had belonged there, with him, our bodies locked together.

I shook my head and swiped at the tears that had formed in my eyes. It was foolish to remember. Maybe later when I was alone and could touch myself, imagine that it was him, but not right now.

Now, all I could think of was the way he looked at me, as if I was his only focus. I wasn't naïve. We had no commitment, nothing between us that suggested we would've been anything more than a one-night stand, but for that one night, he had been with me, only me. He hadn't been thinking of someone else, or using me for his own pleasure.

I could only wonder if the man my parents had chosen for me would be equally as attentive. The knot in the pit of my stomach said he would not. My husband would be chosen for his family, his bloodline, nothing else. My own desires were secondary to what was best for the kingdom, and I'd always known it would be so.

I was, after all, a princess.

Chapter 7

Reed

What the hell just happened?

I stared at the bedroom door as it closed behind Nami. I was still kneeling on the bed, buck naked, the scent of her still on my body long after she'd left with two guys who looked like they should be linebackers in the NFL. It wasn't until I realized that I hadn't gotten rid of the condom that I managed to move. I grimaced as I pulled it off and tossed it into the trashcan. Now I was standing in the middle of the room, still trying to figure out what had happened.

One moment, we'd both been coming down from insanely intense orgasms, and the next minute, I'd been sure I was about to be assaulted by two angry-looking men. I still didn't know what Nami had said to them, only that it had made them leave without hitting me. Not that I wasn't grateful, but it would've been nice to have had some sort of explanation other than the apology Nami had given me.

Who was she? Those men had obviously been her bodyguards, and I supposed it was possible they'd thought I'd been forcing her, but somehow, I thought there was more to it than that. A rich girl might have bodyguards, but I'd gotten the impression that she was more than just someone with money.

I shook my head as I walked into the bathroom and turned on the shower. Tonight had been one of the strangest nights of my life, and one of the best. Most of the other women I'd slept with since coming to Europe had been enjoyable, but Nami had been different. She had an innocence to her without being naïve. A rare combination. And she'd said she was inexperienced, but her body had definitely known what it was doing.

I hissed as the spray hit my back. I'd forgotten that she'd scratched me. From the feel of it, she'd gotten me pretty good. I smiled to myself as I wondered if her nipple hurt. I almost hoped it did. I actually wanted her to remember me, which was strange because every other woman I'd been with, I'd wanted them to forget as soon as they'd left. Hell,

I'd wanted to forget them. I'd enjoyed the sex while we were doing it, but afterwards, I just felt empty, like a part of me was missing and no matter what I did, I couldn't fill it.

Nami, though, I found myself wishing that we could've spent more time together. And not just another go in bed either, which was strange. As good as the sex had been, it would've made complete sense for me to want to take her again, keep her here all night, fucking until neither of us could see straight. That wasn't what I was thinking, however. Well, not the only thing I was thinking.

I actually wanted to spend time with her. Talk to her. Learn what made her tick. Discover what she did for a living or if she was like me, living off of an inheritance. I thought an inheritance, but she'd struck me as the kind of person who didn't spend a lot of time partying. I'd watched her for a bit at the club before I'd approached, deciding if she was the one I wanted to take back to my room. She hadn't exactly looked like she'd been enjoying herself. It was like she was trying to enjoy being there.

As I washed my hair, I wondered what she was rebelling against. Parents? Society? What expectations had driven her to that club? To my bed? I frowned as I realized she might not have come with me because she'd wanted to be with me, but rather because I'd been the one dancing with her when she'd made the decision. I shouldn't have cared. We'd both gotten what we'd wanted: good sex. Okay, great sex. But still, I should've been relieved at the thought of her having only picked me out of convenience rather than actual attraction. I wasn't though. I wanted her to have wanted me. Wanted me as much as I'd wanted her.

And I had wanted her. From the moment I'd seen her, I'd wanted her more than I'd wanted anyone in a long time. Since Piper, as a matter of fact. I reached for my soap and told myself that if I was honest, I'd wanted Nami more than I'd wanted Piper. It had taken a while, but I'd come to see that what Piper had told me before had been true. I'd fallen so hard for her because of what had been going on in my life. I hadn't loved the woman I'd been engaged to and Piper had been there, warm and willing. She'd had a crush on me and we'd both let it convince us that we were supposed to be together. I'd thought I'd loved her, but I knew now that I hadn't. Not really. I'd loved the idea of her, of the freedom she represented.

The other women I'd been with since coming to Europe, they'd all been fun, and while they'd ranged in appearance and had run anywhere from twenty to thirty, they'd all been essentially the same. Sexual, physical beings. Some of them might've been intelligent, but that hadn't been a factor. I'd seen the same expression in all of their eyes. Lust. Whether for money, fame or my body, it didn't matter. They'd just wanted it, wanted me to fuck them, but hadn't wanted to know me. Nami and I hadn't talked much, but it hadn't taken more than a couple seconds with her to know that she was different. Or at least I hoped she was. Hoped that she'd wanted me for me and not for what I could offer her.

I closed my eyes as I stepped under the spray. I needed to stop thinking about her. I was going to Madrid tomorrow morning, leaving France and everything here behind. Besides, she'd said that she had a train to catch in the morning as well. We'd never see each other again.

I dried off as I walked back into the bedroom, tossed the wet towel onto the floor and climbed under the covers. I could smell the two of us on the bedspread and I closed my eyes as my body responded.

As I rolled onto my side, something sharp and hard dug into my ribs. I swore as I sat up, reaching over to turn on the light. There, on the sheets, was a necklace. A thin golden chain with an emerald pendant. I wasn't an expert, but I was willing to bet both metal and jewel were real. An image flashed through my mind. The jewel hanging just above Nami's gorgeous breasts. The necklace must've fallen off when she'd scrambled to cover up when her goons had come in.

I sat there, holding the necklace in my hand and wondered what I should do with it. I had her name, but nothing else to go on, so it wasn't like I could just mail it back to her. I could leave it at the front desk here, but I wasn't sure her bodyguards would be pleased with me for making a public connection between Nami and myself. I knew where she was staying at least. I could go over and give it to the desk clerk there, have him call her room and tell her that someone had found her necklace. A little white lie about where and no one would have to know the truth.

The jewel heated up in my hand, reminding me of the way her skin had heated under my touch, how it had flushed a lovely dusky color. At first, I'd thought she'd just been tan, but when she'd been bare, I'd realized it was just her natural complexion. She was quite the exotic beauty, I thought. The skin and dark hair in stark contrast to her eyes, those bluish-green pools.

I shook my head and flopped onto my back. Damn. Now all I could think about were those eyes, that body. The way she'd looked up at me when I'd been above her, inside her. The tight, wet heat of her molding around me. How our bodies had fit together so perfectly.

"Shit." I squeezed my eyes closed and tried to think of something else, but it was too late. My cock was getting hard at the memory of her. The way she'd tasted. The expression on her face when she'd come.

"Fuck!" I practically yelled it and had a moment to wonder if the room next to mine could hear me. If they could, they definitely would've heard Nami earlier.

I swore again. The memory of how she'd sounded when she'd come that last time made my stomach tighten almost painfully and my already hard cock throb with need. I could try to ignore it, will it to go away with thoughts of unappealing things. I could go to sleep, forget about Nami and head to Madrid in the morning as I'd planned. Leave the necklace with the desk here and not care about whether or not Nami got it back.

I sighed. I couldn't do it. I couldn't forget about

her. I closed my eyes and she was there. Those lips, swollen with rough kisses. That neck I'd wanted to mark. Her breasts, full and perfect. Nipples so responsive to every little touch...

My hand was around my cock before I'd consciously decided to do it. With Nami's necklace in one hand, gem biting into my palm, I began to stroke myself. I thought of her, those silky curls I'd buried my hand in. The thin layer of coarser ones between her legs. Just enough so she wasn't completely bare, but not too much. The way her pussy had clamped down on my fingers when I'd made her come. Her body shuddering against mine when I held her close during her last climax. How it felt to be inside her. Wondering what it would be like to have been bare, skin sliding against skin. Emptying into her, filling her...

I came with a half-groan that was her name, cum spilling over my hand and onto the sheets. I was still breathing heavily as I looked at the necklace again. It was probably a mistake, but the necklace gave me an excuse to do it. After all, I couldn't let her leave without it. It was probably some sort of family heirloom or a gift or something.

My stomach clenched. Maybe a gift from a fiancé. No, I thought, she wouldn't have done that.

She wasn't the type of woman who'd cheat. I pushed aside the thought that I'd done just that, slept with a woman when I'd been engaged to someone else. That had been different. A different set of circumstances. Besides, I thought with a wry smile, Nami was a better person than I was.

I clutched the necklace tighter as I rolled onto my side, away from the damp spot. I'd clean up in the morning. Right now, I needed to sleep. I had a busy day ahead of me. It would be a long-shot, but I had to try to find her. After all, she really did need her necklace back. Anything else would just be icing on the cake.

Chapter 8

Nami

I didn't sleep well at all. If I hadn't been dreaming up some way to get out of the whole arranged marriage thing I knew was coming up as soon as I arrived home, I was replaying every scintillating minute with Reed. Needless to say, I was both tired and frustrated when my alarm went off, and that was just the start of my day. Now I was on a train moving across France, headed for a private airport in Italy where a plane waited to take me back to Saja.

I'd tried calling my father as soon as I'd gotten back to the hotel, thinking I could at least talk him out of bringing me home early, but he hadn't taken my calls. The fact that he'd sent them straight to voicemail told me that he was angry with me, angrier than he'd ever been. He'd never refused to speak to me before.

"Not that it matters," I said out loud. No one else was in the private car so my musings were safe. "What else can he do to me? I already have my degree, so he can no longer hold college over my head. He's already set up my marriage so he can't threaten to marry me off early."

I was sure that the marriage was one of the things he was worried about. If my behavior caused a scandal, a chance existed that the man or his family would call off the engagement. I couldn't say that the idea didn't have its appeal. The fact still remained that it wouldn't matter if this fiancé bolted or not. My parents would simply turn to their second choice and the wedding would continue as scheduled. Someone was always willing to marry a princess, even if they themselves would never get to rule.

I scowled at my reflection in the window, watching the blur of scenery whipping by. Even though my parents wanted me to obey their rules and be the obedient daughter, they'd also raised me to be strong enough to rule the kingdom after they were gone. Part of that strength included not allowing my husband to override me. It was ironic, I thought, how one of the things they'd instilled in me from birth could be the same thing they were trying to suppress. I supposed their intent was for me to be strong-willed, but not against them. I may have been an adult, but to them I was still a child. I assumed it was the same for a lot of parents, but with mine, the difference was that I couldn't do the usual young adult thing of going off to do my own thing, knowing they might not approve but would accept it as a natural part of growing up. Abandoning my parents' wishes would mean walking away from my people, my country, my duty. I would be giving up a legacy that my family had upheld for generations.

And yet, I wondered if it would be worth it. Being able to choose what I wanted to do, how I wanted to live. My fingers touched my lips. Who I wanted to love.

I didn't love Reed. I wasn't a fairy tale princess, falling in love at first sight, but he intrigued me. Something about him called to me and I wished I had the opportunity to explore it.

I'd had that instant click with Aaron, but it had never been romantic, not even when we'd had sex. Sure, he was hot, but even the physical attraction had been different. With him, it had been more of an appreciation of his physique, an admiration. I could appreciate the muscles and his strong, masculine features. It had been that attraction that had made our sexual encounter pleasant, but we'd only ever connected as friends.

I didn't want to be friends with Reed.

I sighed and rested my forehead against the cool glass of the window. It wasn't like I wanted a relationship with Reed. Or maybe I did. I didn't know. But that was something a normal girl would be able to figure out, right? She would be allowed to take her time to get to know a guy she found attractive and amusing. See if he was the kind of man she wanted to be with. Find out what kind of sexual chemistry there was between them.

I snorted a very unladylike laugh and leaned back in my seat. I already knew the answer to that one. The sexual chemistry between us was explosive to say the least. I shifted in my seat, letting myself enjoy the dull ache between my legs. I'd heard the phrase "ridden hard" used when talking about sex, but I'd never had a clear picture of it until last night. Aaron had been gentle, and my body had responded. Reed had, most definitely, not been gentle and I'd enjoyed it even more.

My cheeks flushed at the memory of how he'd used his teeth on me. The first time, I'd been startled, but the zing of electricity racing through me had been something much different than pain, something more intense than any of Aaron's kisses or touches had been. All I'd known at the time was that I'd wanted more.

Now, I wondered how Reed had known something about me that I hadn't. How had this complete stranger been able to play my body with his fingers and mouth? How had he known that I would beg him to fuck me harder than I would've thought enjoyable? Reed had seemed like a man who had known many women, but Aaron had known both woman and men. Why had Reed been the one to truly show me what sex could be like?

I felt tears pricking at my eyelids and I rubbed my palms against my eyes. Now that I knew, could I be satisfied by anything else? What would I do if my future husband didn't understand me the way that Reed had? Would he allow me to teach him, show him what I liked? But would that reveal my secret? I could explain away certain biological things fairly easily. Saja wasn't so primitive that they would expect a woman's hymen to be intact, especially if that woman had spent a good part of her teenage years taking riding lessons. It would be the sworn statements of my bodyguards, my parents and myself that would be held as testimony to my virginity. But if I showed myself to be knowledgeable of what I liked, would my husband assume I had simply learned while pleasuring myself, or would he suspect the truth?

I couldn't be put in prison or executed for having lost my virginity before marriage. That wasn't how my country did things. Most Saja men and women engaged in premarital sex just as those in civilized places did. My virginity was only important because of what it meant to the man I was supposed to marry. If he – whoever he was – found out the truth, he could divorce me, and collect a hearty settlement for breach of contract, thanks to the papers we all had to sign. That was to say nothing of the scandal it would cause. Like the rest of the world, Saja citizens loved to gossip, especially about celebrities, and in my country, no one was a bigger celebrity than royalty.

I ran my hands through my short curls and nearly growled in frustration. Why couldn't I have been born somewhere else, to some other family? While I'd loved my time in America as well as what I'd seen of Europe, I'd never intended to stay away from Saja. I loved my home, my beautiful island. I loved my people. Unlike some royal families, we weren't kept quite so separate from everyone else, weren't taught that we were better than the common people. Sure, I'd had a bodyguard even there, but it hadn't been like college. They had been my people. No real danger there. But still, the line had been there, the separation of knowing who I was and who they were.

"Why couldn't I have been born to someone else? Some other family," I spoke my thoughts out loud, needing to hear them. Needing to hear myself actually wish that I wasn't me. "I could be normal."

I laughed softly. Normal. It sounded as funny out loud as it had in my head. Other girls dreamed about being princesses, but I dreamed about being other girls. But even as I said the words, I'd known I didn't really wish them to be true. That's why I'd needed to hear it. To let myself know how ludicrous it sounded. Wanting to be something I wasn't, shirking my duty.

Sometimes though, I did wonder if things would've been different if any of the three children my parents had lost between my sister and I had lived. One would have been a son, the other two, we didn't know. If I'd had a brother who'd lived, I supposed things might have been different. I would have had a choice then. I could have given up my position as the eldest to him, let him be king and have lived my life as a princess like my sister. Still not quite a regular person, but with more freedom than I currently had.

I supposed, technically, I could have abdicated the throne in favor of my little sister. Halea was only sixteen. She'd have years before my parents would make her marry, and she was a much more compliant child than I'd ever been. She would do as she was told.

And that was why I never could've done it. No matter how much I longed to be free of the responsibilities that came with being the crown princess, I would never have put my sister in my place. Not because I wanted the power, but because I knew what it would do to her. She wouldn't just be bendable to our parents' wishes, but also to whomever she married. She would be queen in name only. It would be too easy for a man to take over, and I didn't know of any man on Saja who could be trusted with that responsibility and honor.

No, I would do my duty. Return home without complaint. I'd take over the responsibilities required of me. I'd marry the man they chose. I would be queen, the strong queen that Saja deserved.

With the choice made, all I had to do now was wait. The train would be in Italy soon and it wouldn't be long after that, I'd be on a plane home. I closed my eyes and leaned my head back. Maybe I could get some sleep before it all happened.

I must have drifted at some point because I sat up with a start when the door to the car opened. I opened my mouth to ask my bodyguards what was wrong, but the words died before they came out. It wasn't Tomas or Kai who stood in the doorway.

It was Reed.

Chapter 9

Reed

It hadn't been easy, finding the right train. I'd ended up having to bribe someone to tell me what train Nami's tickets were for, and then I'd had to trade mine for Madrid for ones to Venice, all while watching the clock and hoping I'd be able to make it in time. I'd had to run, but I'd gotten there before the train had pulled out. Then it had just been a matter of finding the right car. I'd started at the far end of the train and worked my way up. I didn't think she'd be in any of the more public cars, but I wasn't about to miss her because I didn't search thoroughly enough.

At first, I'd told myself that I would just find her and give her the necklace. Then I'd apologize for freezing the other night and give her a proper good-bye. When I traded my ticket, I told myself that it was because I needed to get onto the train to find her. I didn't let myself think of anything beyond that.

When I saw the two big guys standing in front of the door to a private car, I knew I'd found her. There was no way either of those two would let me in, which meant I had to figure out a way to distract them. I wasn't sure what made me think to do it, but I stepped back into the dinner car and leaned over to speak to the man behind the bar. Two minutes later, a pair of men in suits hurried past me to investigate the possible terrorists I might have seen talking in the hallway.

I opened the door, and for a moment, thought I'd been wrong, that the car was empty. Then I saw her and my heart skipped a beat. She was sleeping for a split second before she sensed that someone was here and bolted upright. She opened her mouth and I thought she would say something or scream, but I watched the recognition dawn in her eyes a moment before they widened in surprise.

"Hi." That came out a lot less impressive than I'd imagined it would be.

"Hello." She recovered quickly. "I did not expect to ever see you again."

I leaned against the doorframe and held up my hand, letting the necklace drop. The emerald bounced on the end. "You forgot something."

Her cheeks flushed and my stomach tightened at the memory of that same flush covering her entire body. She started to stand and I held up a hand, walking towards her. When I was just a couple steps away, the car lurched and my confident swagger ended up with me tumbling onto the seat across from her.

I swore as I fell, face flaming. Could I look any more idiotic? I'd been prepared to give her the necklace and make a suave exit so that the last memory she had of me was a scorching kiss and not me kneeling on the bed, naked, and staring at the two massive, angry men who'd just burst in. Instead, she had her hands over her mouth, unsuccessfully attempting to stifle a laugh.

"Are you okay?" she managed to ask as I attempted to right myself.

I nodded. "Just embarrassed," I muttered. I got to my feet and held out the necklace. "Here."

She stood and smiled up at me, her eyes sparkling with humor. She took the necklace, her fingers brushing against mine. Electricity shot up my arm. Suddenly, the air felt thicker and I was aware of everything. The way her hair curled across her forehead. The curve of her breast and hip beneath her clothes. The clean, fresh scent of her.

"I—" The word stuck and I cleared my throat before trying again. "I'll be going."

I was two steps from the door when she spoke. "Wait."

I stopped but didn't turn back to her.

"Do you have to go?" Her voice was soft.

"Well, um, it might be a good idea if I leave before your bodyguards come back." I glanced over my shoulder.

"Where did they go?" She sounded more amused than scared which told me the bodyguards weren't there for protection from a specific threat, but rather a lifestyle thing.

"Someone may or may not have reported two suspicious looking people lingering in the hallway, and may or may not have said they overheard something that sounded like a conversation about a bomb."

Her eyes widened and, for a moment, I thought she would go off on me. Instead, she laughed. "You really did that to them?"

I turned to face her, sticking my hands in my pockets in what I hoped was a nonchalant manner. "I may or may not have."

She shook her head and gestured towards the

seats. "Oh, they will be angry, but they won't come in here. Not when they know I'm pissed at them for..." She blushed, but kept her chin up, "what happened last night."

"So, what you're saying is that I'm safer in here than I am out there?" I grinned. Whatever this spark was between us, I liked it.

"Most definitely." Her tone was serious, but her eyes were twinkling. "So why don't you sit and keep me company."

I took the seat across from her again, not wanting to presume what she meant by keeping her company. One part of my body was sure of what it wanted and I attempted to subtly adjust myself as I settled in the seat.

"We didn't really talk much yesterday," she said with a smile.

I was pleased to see that she looked as nervous as I was. "Well, there were plenty of words and sounds, but I don't really think that constituted talking."

Her blush darkened. "I didn't even get to ask where you were from."

I smiled. "Philadelphia. And you?"

Her face stiffened, smile freezing.

"Never mind." I quickly changed the subject.

Since I was desperate for another subject, I said the first thing that popped into my head. "I have to ask, did you go with me last night because I was convenient?" I immediately regretted the question as soon as it was out of my mouth. "Sorry, didn't mean to put you on the spot. Again."

"No," she said. Her expression softened. "I went with you because I liked you."

I was surprised at how relieved I felt at that simple statement, but I couldn't stop myself from asking a follow up question. "You didn't know me. How did you know you liked me?"

She frowned and my curiosity piqued. "It's hard to explain."

"Try." I gave her my best charming smile and tried not to sound eager.

"Well, I thought you were handsome, of course, and an excellent dancer." She turned her head, like she couldn't continue when she was looking at me. "But it was the way I felt when you touched me."

"Like little sparks of electricity dancing across your skin?" I asked softly.

She turned back towards me, her eyes meeting mine. "Exactly."

We were both silent for a minute and I supposed she was thinking the same thing I was, how this had suddenly become something more than a random hook up. I didn't know what it was, but it was something.

She leaned back, breaking eye contact. "So, Mr. Philadelphia, what brought you to Paris?"

I sat back as well. I didn't mind that she was deliberately moving the subject away from our connection. Whatever it was, it was intense, and I didn't blame her for wanting to dial it back a bit.

"I'm taking a vacation," I said. "A bit of a European tour."

She crossed her arms and raised an eyebrow. "Really? You don't have a job to go home to? A...family?"

The way she said it made it pretty clear she wasn't asking about my parents and siblings. I smiled and mimicked her posture. "I worked for my family business since I got out of college and I recently realized that I didn't want to do it anymore. Decided to take a bit of a break." I felt myself relaxing, enjoying the interaction. "As for my family, my parents aren't exactly pleased with me at the moment and my spoiled little sister is trying to prove that she has what it takes to fill my shoes." I tried to keep my tone light, but a slight narrowing of Nami's eyes told me that I hadn't succeeded as well as I would've liked.

"Parents can be funny," she said. The tone of her voice made me think that she wasn't talking about just mine. Her eyes flicked away and back again. "I have a younger sister too." She smiled. "But she's not spoiled."

I chuckled. "That's good. How old is she?" I was actually fishing for a hint about her own age, but didn't want to come out and ask it. Sometimes she looked like she was barely out of high school, other times she appeared years older.

"Sixteen." Her lips twitched in humor. "Six years younger than me. That's what you wanted to know, isn't it?"

I shrugged, grinning at her. "Aren't you going to ask me how old I am?"

She shook her head.

"So you're not worried you slept with an old man?"

She laughed. "You're not even thirty yet."

"Good guess," I said. "Twenty-seven." Something clicked for me as I did the math. "Is this a graduation trip?"

"Good guess," she echoed me with a smile. "Princeton."

"Nice," I said. "Columbia."

"Political science with a minor in classical literature."

"MBA."

"Let me guess," she said. "Parents?"

I nodded. "And yours?"

"Not the minor," she said. "That's all me."

"Well, you did better than me," I admitted. "I didn't manage to get a minor I liked."

"Maybe that's what I liked about you," she said. "It seems we're kindred spirits."

My stomach clenched at her words. It wasn't like she was saying we were soulmates or destined to be together forever, anything like that, which was good, but she was saying there was a deeper connection here.

"Well, there's one way to find out." This time it was me who guided the conversation away from the serious. "Favorite color?"

"Scarlet." She grinned.

"Cyan." The word popped out and I flushed as I glanced at her eyes. I'd always liked blue and green, but if I'd been asked before what my favorite color was, I would've said silver. I hurried to ask another question. "Favorite food?"

"Apple pie."

"Pizza. With extra cheese and pepperoni."

"My turn for a question." Nami's eyes were glittering with something I couldn't quite place. "Girlfriend?"

"No. You?"

"No girlfriend. Or boyfriend." Her tongue teased her bottom lip and my blood began to run south.

I tried to get my mind back to something more innocent and the back and forth conversation continued. Favorite song. Favorite movie. Childhood pets. School subject. It kept going until Nami stood up suddenly and walked over to the door. I thought she was going to look out and see if her bodyguards were back, but she didn't. Instead, she turned the lock.

When she turned back to me, her eyes were dark. "One more question. And please answer honestly."

I nodded.

"Do you want me?"

Chapter 10

Reed

Was she kidding?

Did I want her? There was no way in this life I didn't want her. All confusing connection shit aside, she was gorgeous and a great lay. I would've had to be dead not to want her.

I stood up as she walked back over to her seat. I reached out and grabbed her hand, stopping her from sitting down. "I want you." I traced along her jaw with my finger. "Do you really need to ask?"

A shadow crossed her face and I saw a hint of vulnerability in her eyes.

"You do, don't you?" I said softly. I brushed her hair back from her face and then ran my thumb along her bottom lip. She shivered and her response made my chest tighten. "How could I not want you? You're the singularly most exquisite thing I've ever seen. I haven't been able to stop thinking about you."

"I've been thinking about you, too," she admitted, her voice quiet, eyes down.

"Look at me." My tone was neither harsh nor loud, but she immediately obeyed, her eyes rising to meet mine. "Do you want me?"

She pushed herself up on her toes so that she could touch her lips to mine. It was barely even a kiss, but it sent a bolt of electricity straight through me. She put her hands on my chest and leaned her body into mine, the motion of the train causing us to sway together. "I want you," she whispered.

My hands went to her waist, holding her as I bent my head to give her a proper kiss. Her arms slid up around my neck as I parted her lips with my tongue, thoroughly exploring her mouth. I slipped my hands under her shirt, keeping one at the small of her back while the other moved up her spine. I paused at her bra strap but didn't undo it. I knew where I wanted things to end up, but I also didn't want to presume. Her fingers twisted in my hair and she pressed her belly more firmly against my hips until I moaned. I was already half-hard and the memory of what it had been like inside her was quickly changing half to full.

She stepped back, breaking the kiss, and I let

her go. I'd be disappointed if that's all there was, but it had been a hell of a kiss. She grabbed the bottom of her short-sleeved shirt and pulled it over her head. While I was getting rid of my own clothes, she stripped off her jeans and undergarments so that by the time I was completely naked, she was too.

"Sit."

I did as she asked. No way was I going to argue with a beautiful naked woman.

"I wanted to do this last night," she said as she walked over to me.

I swallowed hard as she went to her knees, pushing my knees apart to make room for her. Her breasts brushed against my thighs and her nipples hardened at the contact. A surge of desire went through me. She was so beautiful.

When her hand wrapped around my cock, I groaned. Her tongue flicked against the tip, then circled it, making every nerve in my sensitive skin light up. As her lips closed over it and she took me into the moist heat of her mouth, I swore. She'd said she hadn't had much experience, but she definitely had some great instincts. Her tongue was moving around and across the part of me that was in her mouth while her hand stroked the several inches she couldn't take. I gripped the edge of the seat as she dropped further down, her lips stretching wide around me. When her free hand reached underneath me to cup my balls, my entire body jerked, pushing my cock even deeper into her mouth. She drew back as her fingers began to toy with me, rolling and massaging my balls even as she ran her tongue up and down my length.

Finally, I had to call her off. "No more." My voice was rough.

She glanced towards the door. "It's too bad we don't have hours more because I would very much like to taste you."

Fuck. I took her chin in my hand and pulled her up to me, sitting up to capture her mouth. I could taste the salt from my skin and it only fueled my desire. She climbed up onto my lap, her knees resting on either side of my waist. I grabbed her hips, wanting nothing more than to sink inside her, feel her gripping me tight, but safety always came first.

"Condom," I managed to say.

She caught my bottom lip between her teeth, nibbling at it before sucking it into her mouth.

Inexperienced my ass. This girl knew what she was doing. Either that or she had some amazing instincts.

"Got it," she said.

I gave her a questioning look as she tore open the packet.

"I took a couple from the hotel before I went to the club the other night," she explained as she rolled the latex over my throbbing cock. "I hadn't planned anything, but I figured it was better to be prepared."

"You would've made quite the Boy Scout," I muttered. I circled one of her nipples with my finger. "Except the whole being a girl thing."

"Reed."

I looked up as she said my name.

"I want to see you."

I didn't have to ask what she meant because she started to lower herself onto me. Myriad emotions played across her face as she took me inch by agonizing inch until she was on my lap, every bit of me buried inside her. She rocked back and forth, her eyes closing, head falling forward. My fingers tightened on her hips until I was sure I would leave marks.

"Does it always feel like this?"

Her question surprised me, distracting me from the urgent need to move. "Like what?"

Her eyes locked with mine as she slowly began to rise. "I cannot put it into words." Her accent had thickened. "Do you not know what I mean?"

I did. I hadn't at first because her question had caught me off guard, but then I'd gotten it. Sex with her wasn't like sex with any of the other women I'd hooked up with during my trip. Our bodies moved together like we'd done this a thousand times before, but not in the way that it was old or something like that. More like a dance that we both knew the steps to and we moved at the same rhythm.

"No," I admitted. "It's not always like this."

I leaned forward, moving one hand to capture her breast. I squeezed the firm flesh as she picked up the pace. When I latched onto her nipple with my mouth, she cried out something in another language. Judging by the way her body tightened, I assumed it was positive. My tongue circled her nipple, teased the hard point of it. When I began to suck on it, her body jerked against mine, driving me deeper than I would've thought possible.

"Reed," she gasped my name. "Reed, please."

Her nails dug into my shoulders and I knew without her saying what she needed. I pulled her down on me hard, making her whimper, and then bit the delicate flesh in my mouth. I felt her mouth on my neck, her teeth in my skin even as she cried out, using my body to muffle the sound. I held her, thrusting up into her twice, pushing her through her orgasm as my own exploded through me. She wrapped her legs around me, our bodies still intimately joined as we rode out our pleasure.

I kissed the side of her neck as my hand ran up and down her spine. I'd answered honestly when I'd told her that it wasn't always like this, but I hadn't told her that I didn't know why, or that it scared me half to death. I could feel whatever this was between us growing. It didn't matter that we barely knew each other. This thing was completely out of our control, and I knew that if we didn't walk away soon, we'd have started something that neither of us had intended.

A knock at the door made both of us jump, ending the moment.

"What is it?" Nami called out, not trying to hide the annoyance in her voice.

"We are almost in Venice."

She looked at me and sighed. "Very well, Tomas." She climbed off of my lap, grimacing as I slid out of her. She spoke to me, her voice low, "You need to go."

I looked at the door and then back at her. "And how do you suggest I do that? I seriously doubt your buddies out there will let me walk out. It doesn't take a rocket scientist to figure what we were doing in here."

She frowned as she reached for her clothes. "You're right."

She opened a door, revealing a tiny private bathroom. She wet a washcloth and handed it to me before taking one for herself. We cleaned ourselves up in silence and dressed. We hadn't had the chance for this sort of awkward moment last night, but it wasn't as strained as I'd thought it would've been. I could tell she was thinking and I left her alone, my own thoughts preoccupied with what I was going to do now.

"Hide in the bathroom," she said suddenly.

"What?" I asked, surprised and wondering how that was a solution.

"Hide in the bathroom," she repeated. "I'll ask Tomas and Kai to come in and get my luggage, then take it to the last car and wait for me. I'll make up something about wanting to avoid the press."

"Press?"

The tips of her ears turned pink and I knew she wasn't just flushed from sex. She kept her back to me as she answered, "My father is making me come home early because the media took a picture of me at the club yesterday."

100

"You weren't allowed to be at a club? You're over twenty-one." I found myself wondering again who she was.

She took a deep breath and turned around to face me. "My parents have a very strict code of behavior that I am supposed to follow." She gestured towards the door. "They're supposed to keep me in line."

I grinned. "I don't think they've been doing a very good job."

"You have no idea." She didn't seem amused. "This trip was a graduation present from my parents. I was allowed to have fun, but only the sort of fun of which they would approve. Dancing at a club was not on the list."

"What do they have against dancing?" I asked. Was she from some sort of strict religious family?

"Nothing," she said. "But it is what might come after the dancing that is the problem." One side of her mouth tipped upwards in a half-smile. "What did happen after we danced?"

My eyes widened. "Sex?" Shit. What had I gotten myself into?

"Sex." She nodded. "Tomas and Kai's main job watching me through college and on this trip was to keep me from having sex." Now she grinned at me.

"As you can see, that didn't work very well."

"Will you be in trouble?" I asked, concern for her superseding anything else.

She shrugged. "Not if they keep their mouths shut, and since it would mean admitting they didn't do their job, I don't think they'll say anything. And it's not like I'll be in danger if my parents find out."

"Nami," I began.

She put her hand on my arm. "Don't worry about me, Reed. The worst that will happen is that I'll receive a lecture on proper behavior for...the way a lady should act."

I was pretty sure she'd been planning on saying something else, but I didn't push.

Her smile was sad now. "I just wanted a few days to do what I wanted, not what was expected of me."

I could definitely sympathize with that.

"I wanted to have fun without constantly having to wonder about what everyone else would think." She scowled at the door. "Without those two hovering over me every minute of every day."

An idea popped into my head. It was a bad one, possibly the worst one I'd ever had, and I knew I should just keep my mouth shut. But Nami looked so miserable and I couldn't help but compare her to me. She was where I'd been back in Philadelphia, bound by her parents' expectations without a hope of breaking free. I couldn't do anything about that, but I could offer her what she'd just said she wanted.

"Are you serious about wanting to have some fun?" I asked.

She looked up at me, a puzzled expression on her face. "Yes."

"And you want to get away from the linebackers out there?"

She nodded.

"You promise you won't be in any danger if you do something reckless?" I didn't want to risk this if it meant she would be hurt.

"I won't," she said. "My family has expectations, but they aren't violent if those aren't met."

"Then call them in here. I'll hide while you have them carry the luggage to the last car like you'd said. Except, instead of me sneaking out and away, we're going to go together."

Chapter 11

Nami

I stared at him, unsure if I was hearing him correctly. Surely he couldn't be suggesting that the two of us run away together. That was ludicrous. And yet a part of me was thrilled at the idea.

I immediately pushed the thought aside. He didn't mean for us to run away together. Not like that. Besides, I couldn't do it, couldn't leave my family. But...I realized what he meant. A little detour before going home. A chance to have what I'd wanted, at least a single day of freedom. A day to have fun without Tomas and Kai breathing down my neck, watching my every move.

"What do you say?" He held out a hand. "Want to have some fun before you head home?"

I couldn't begin to say all the ways this was a bad idea. The risk to my reputation, being out and about with a virtual stranger. The chance that my parents would find out. The ruining of the engagement.

Still, I couldn't help but think about what it would be like, to walk around Venice with Reed, like we were some couple on a romantic getaway. No eyes on me, no worrying about every little thing.

Before I could second-guess myself, I slid my hand into his. "Yes," I said. "I'd like that very much."

He raised my hand and kissed the back of it. "Then let's get started. We should be arriving in Venice soon." He released my hand and went into the bathroom, closing the door behind him.

I took a moment to collect myself and check to make sure my clothes were all on properly. I didn't want to risk them thinking there was anything strange going on. I needed them to think that I was still going along with my father's wishes. They wouldn't force me to do anything. It wasn't like that. But they would stay by my side the whole time, make sure I was never alone. Use their presence to intimidate crowds to move around us so that I could only go where they wanted me to go. They could call my father, tell him that I'd tried to slip away...again. He wouldn't hurt me or anything like that. What he wouldn't do was trust me again.

"Tomas, Kai." I opened the door and gave them

each a quick smile. "Come here please."

They both looked angry and, if what Reed had said was true, they had good reason to be. Neither of them said anything though. They wouldn't. Being detained wasn't exactly the kind of thing security would be pleased to tell their employer. They came in without a word or a greeting, but that wasn't entirely unusual.

"I want to get off from the last car," I informed them. "Avoid the possibility of any media."

They exchanged looks that I recognized. They didn't generally like it when I took charge. They preferred to follow things like class schedules, itineraries, things like that. They were loyal though, understood their role when it came to who was in charge. They would do what I asked unless it went directly against my father's orders.

"Take the luggage to the car and wait for me there."

"But, Pr–"

"Are you really going to argue?" I cut Tomas off before he could call me by my title. I didn't know how much Reed could hear, but I didn't want him hearing that. "It's a simple task. Take our luggage to the last train car and I'll meet you there when we arrive in Venice."

"Shouldn't we not wait until we arrive at the station, take our things then and go together?" Kai suggested.

I shook my head. "Do you really think it's a good idea to try to haul all of our luggage through crowded corridors while everyone else is trying to leave too?"

They exchanged looks again and this time I knew it was because I'd made a good point. I honestly hadn't even thought about it until I'd said it, but it actually made sense. It seemed that luck was on my side.

"Hurry up." I motioned towards the suitcases and then stepped off to the side to let them pass by. I backed up against the bathroom door so that neither of them would accidentally bump against it. Since it was one of the few places I could be out of the way, it didn't look suspicious.

I closed the door behind them as they left, but didn't tell Reed to come out yet. I wanted to be sure Tomas and Kai didn't come back for something they missed, so I waited a few minutes and then started to open the door. My hand was on the latch before I thought better of it. I didn't want to be rude. I rapped my fingers against the door twice.

"They're gone."

He slid the door aside and we were suddenly face to face. A mere inch apart, I could feel the heat of him, smell the scent of the train's soap mingled with the scent that I recognized as him. I looked up at him, my heart beating hard in my chest.

He cupped my chin, his skin burning against mine. I barely had a moment to register the kiss before his mouth was hard against mine. A shiver of desire went through me as my lips molded themselves to his. My body leaned against his and I could feel him getting hard against my hip.

His teeth scraped my bottom lip and I moaned. I couldn't believe how good he made me feel. A single kiss and my knees were weak.

He sighed as he broke the kiss, but he didn't let me go. "I wish this was a much longer ride."

"Regretting your offer?" I teased. I knew what he meant, but I didn't want to go there. I was already pushing what was smart. There couldn't be anything between us and I could feel us getting closer the longer we were together.

"Getting cold feet, are we?" He smiled at me as he laced his fingers through mine.

"Not a chance." I smiled at him. "You're stuck with me."

His eyes darkened and he squeezed my hand.

"Sounds like fun to me."

Silence fell between us, thick and tense with desire. How could I want him again? I'd slept with Aaron and enjoyed it well enough, but I hadn't wanted him a second time. With Reed, I'd had him twice and still, I wanted more. If I had my way, we'd be heading straight to a hotel and not coming out for a week.

Dammit. I seriously needed to stop thinking about sex with Reed. We weren't going there. We were going to be in Venice and I fully intended to see it.

"How do we do this?" I asked, breaking the moment. "Tomas and Kai will wait in the last car for a while, but I wouldn't put it past them for one to stay with the luggage and the other to come back and get me."

"Then I guess we'd better move then." He dropped a wink and opened the car door. He looked both ways, then pulled me out into the hall after him.

"Where are we going?" I kept my voice low, then flushed when I realized what I was doing.

Reed didn't seem to have noticed because he answered my question in a voice almost as quiet. "The dining car."

"Really?" I asked.

"We'll follow people out of there into one of the other cars and get lost in the shuffle."

"You think that'll work?" I gave him a doubtful look.

He shrugged. "Saw it work in a movie once." He frowned. "At least I think it worked."

I wasn't entirely sure if he was joking or not, but either way, I would go along with it. What was the worst that could happen?

As we made our way into the dining car and ducked into a booth, my stomach was in knots and my palms were sweating. I almost wanted to let go of Reed's hand, but I was more worried that I'd end up losing him in a crowd and then I'd be lost and by myself. I spoke several languages, but wasn't fluent in Italian. I hadn't realized how much I'd accepted the presence of my bodyguards until I thought about what would happen if Reed and I got separated.

"Are you okay?" Reed looked over at me, concern on his face.

I nodded.

"Because you're kind of hurting my hand."

I flushed and let go. He smiled at me as he flexed his fingers and shook his hand.

"Sorry," I muttered.

"Are you sure you're alright?"

"I was just...worried that we'd get separated."

Reed stood and held out his hand. "Don't worry. I won't let you go."

My stomach twisted at his words and I warned myself not to read too much into what he'd said. He was talking about right now, that was all.

I took his hand and let him lead me into the group of people who were heading back to their seats. Even though I knew the chances of Tomas or Kai finding me so quickly were slim, I couldn't stop myself from looking over my shoulder. I had a feeling that wasn't going to change until we were safely outside and deep in the city.

As we stood near the door, Reed pulled me closer to him. "Ready to have some fun?"

I smiled up at him. Despite the nerves, I was starting to feel a rush of excitement, the kind of rush that came from doing something I wasn't supposed to. The best part about all of this, however, wasn't what I was about to do, or even how attracted I was to Reed. The best part was that Reed didn't know who I was, what I was, and he wanted to do this with me. He wanted me for me. Maybe most of it was for my body, but I knew there had to be at least a little part of him that liked me for more than sex, otherwise we wouldn't be here. For the first time in my life, I wasn't a princess or an heir to a throne. I was Nami. Just Nami. And I had a feeling I was going to like it.

Chapter 12

Reed

I couldn't believe I made the offer, and I was even more surprised that she'd accepted. The words had just kind of popped out and then I had to figure out what we were going to do. Fortunately, I was able to put the time I spent in the bathroom to good use. By the time she told me to come out, I had an idea of what to do to get off the train without being seen by her bodyguards. Then she'd been right there and I'd kissed her. I'd needed to kiss her. It wasn't like anything I could explain, only that with her standing that close, I couldn't help myself. The scent of her, the heat of her body.

I shook my head to clear it. I believed Nami when she said her bodyguards wouldn't hurt her. I wasn't so sure they wouldn't hurt me, however. I had a feeling I'd just missed getting the shit beat out of me in my hotel room. I was quite certain it would be in my best interest to avoid them altogether, and to do that, I needed a clear head. Unfortunately, with Nami so close by, it wasn't as easy as I would have liked. I couldn't believe how easily she distracted me.

"When the doors open, just walk right out. Don't rush or keep looking over your shoulder. We're just two tourists coming in to Venice on the train." I kept my voice low.

"More knowledge from movies?" she asked. I could hear a bit of strain in her voice, but there was excitement too.

I couldn't deny that I felt the same. It wasn't like this was some sort of rescue or anything like that. I was just trying to give someone a day or two of freedom and fun because I knew what it was like to live a life for someone else. Part of me wanted to tell her to break free completely, to not wait as long as I did, but I reminded myself that I didn't know Nami's whole story. I couldn't assume that her situation was like mine. I had to trust her to do what was right for her.

Besides, I wasn't a hero. I allowed myself a wry smile. I was an unemployed rich kid making my way across Europe, sleeping with whoever I happened to find. I had no direction, no purpose. In fact, standing here with Nami, getting ready to sneak off a train and vanish into Venice for a day or so, was the first time I'd had a plan beyond the times stamped on my train tickets.

The doors opened and we followed the crowd out. It was almost noon and a beautiful May day in Italy. Nami was gripping my hand tight enough for it almost to hurt, but I didn't say anything this time. Excitement was quickly chasing away my nerves. I led us towards the front of the train, hopefully away from where the bodyguards would be coming once they figured out Nami was gone.

Still, we needed to get away from the station and out of sight. I'd been to Venice once on a business trip, and while I hadn't had time to thoroughly explore the city, I did know a couple places. The first thing we needed, however, was a boat. It wasn't that difficult to find a gondola. Once we settled in, I spoke to the nice Italian man smiling at us. "*Portaci al Museo Guggenheim, per favore.*"

"What was that?" Nami asked. "I caught part of it, but Italian isn't my strongest language."

"I asked him to take us to the Guggenheim Museum," I said. I released her hand and put my arm around her shoulders, pulling her close to me. "Now let's just look like we're enjoying the romance of the city."

I nuzzled the back of her ear to make her laugh and it worked. I felt the last of the tension leave her as she turned towards me, her mouth covering mine. I made a sound of surprise as her tongue pushed between my lips. She turned her body towards me so that her breasts pushed against my chest, her kiss aggressive. My body began to respond and it was only the gondolier clearing his throat that kept me from taking things further.

"Young lovers?" His English was heavily accented but understandable. "From America, no?"

"Yes." I gave him a charming smile. No need for Nami to tell him where she was from. A pair of Americans wouldn't attract that much attention. If Nami was from some place exotic, it might.

"I feel like I'm in a movie," Nami said quietly as we settled back into more appropriate positions. "Something like *Roman Holiday*."

"That's the one with Audrey Hepburn, right?" I asked. "I think I had to watch it in school once."

She rolled her eyes. "You Americans can't even appreciate your finest accomplishments."

I laughed. "Sorry. I'm a bit more of an action adventure kind of guy than the classics."

"Ah, like the adventure we are on now."

I kissed her nose. "Exactly."

What was I doing? Acting like this was some cute little date? I'd always come across as suave and sophisticated. I didn't get women by being goofy or silly. I was charming. Cool, collected. A bit cocky.

Except around her. I'd been all those things yesterday, but today, I'd lost it. I found myself at a loss for words. Fell over my feet. And she seemed to like it. The odd thing was, I sort of did too. It was strange. I felt more relaxed around Nami than I had around any other woman I'd ever been with. Even Piper.

We pulled up next to the museum and I helped Nami up onto the sidewalk. We kept holding hands as we walked into the museum. I'd never been inside, but I figured this would be the best place to hide for a bit. Her bodyguards would have to search for her alone unless they wanted to make a scene by calling the cops and the impression I'd gotten from Nami was that no one wanted attention. Venice was full of places like this and the chances of them finding us right away were slim.

"You know," Nami said quietly. "If I wanted to tour museums, I could've done that with Tomas and Kai."

"Ah," I said. "But could they give you running

commentary about European Abstractionism or one of Jackson Pollock's greatest masterpieces?"

She raised an eyebrow. "You learned about art while getting your MBA?"

"Nope." I grinned at her. "Learned it to impress girls. Did it work?"

She laughed, then slapped a hand over her mouth as the sound echoed. "I think that's one of the things I always hated about these places. I love the beauty of the art work, but I always feel like I'm in church, like I can't talk too loud or I'll be reprimanded."

"I know what you mean," I said, pitching my voice just as low. "And you know what?" I pulled Nami through a door that said 'Employees Only.' "It's always made me want to do something a bit...wicked."

I shut the door behind us and pulled her to me. I couldn't say what it was, but I couldn't keep my hands off her. My mouth was hard on hers and she made a noise that sent my blood rushing south. I cupped her breast through her shirt while the other hand moved down to her ass. She ground her hips against me and it was my turn to moan. The things this woman did to me.

She pushed me back against the door and

moved her mouth from mine, trailing kisses down my neck, pausing at the base to lightly nip at the skin. Her hand slid between us and she pressed her palm against my cock.

"Dammit, Nami," I groaned. If she kept that up, I was either going to end up with a massive hard-on when we walked out of here or I was going to embarrass myself and come in my pants. Neither option was appealing.

"I think I should help you with this little problem." She grinned at me. "Or...not so little."

I stared at her as she went down on her knees. When I'd pulled her in here, I'd imagined making out, copping a feel over her clothes. Not this.

"What are you doing?" The question was ludicrous, but I couldn't stop myself from asking it.

"Having fun." She winked at me as her hands quickly undid my pants, pulling them down just enough for her to reach into my underwear and pull out my cock.

I was already mostly hard, but the moment her lips touched me, that changed. My hands curled into fists as she took half of me, letting me swell in her mouth until she had to release me.

"Nami."

"Shh," she said, her hand running up and down

121

my length. "We don't want anyone coming in here, do we?" She looked up at me, hints of cyan peeking through her thick lashes. "Unless that's what you want." She flicked out her tongue against the tip of my cock and it twitched.

The mental image of what someone would see if they came in flashed through my mind. This beautiful woman on her knees, hand and mouth on my cock. It was gone as quickly as it came, the wet heat of Nami's mouth driving away all coherent thoughts.

I put my hand on her head, not to control her, but needing to touch her. Her curls were soft against my fingers, the sensation adding to what I was feeling as she began to suck on my cock, deep, steady pulls of her mouth that had my knees weak and my pulse racing.

"Nami." I twisted my fingers in her curls. "I'm close."

She looked up at me as my cock slid from between her lips. "I want you to go in my mouth."

I swore. Where had this woman come from?

"Is there a reason why you shouldn't?"

I shook my head.

"Unless you don't want to?" Her voice was soft, uncertain.

I dropped my hand from her head and ran my thumb along her slightly swollen lips. "You have no idea how much I want to."

She took the tip of my thumb in her mouth, sucking on it hard before releasing it. I rested my hand on her cheek as she leaned forward to wrap her lips around me again. My eyes closed, head falling back against the door with a thunk. Some women had a natural affinity for things of a primal nature. Nami had to be one of those because the things she was doing with her mouth and tongue...

My entire body stiffened as I came. I bit down on my bottom lip to stifle the sounds I wanted to make. My cock pulsed in her mouth, emptying even as her hand continued to work over the base, milking out every last drop. I could feel her swallowing and forced my eyes open. I looked down to find her eyes already on me, watching as she licked me clean.

I reached down and grabbed her arms, pulling her to her feet a bit more roughly than I'd intended.

"My turn." The words were practically a growl and her eyes darkened at the sound.

I turned her so she was facing the door and quickly opened her pants. She gasped as I shoved my hand down beneath her panties. Her legs parted as my fingers slid between her folds.

"I wish you were wearing a skirt," I said, my voice low. I pressed my mouth against her ear. "Because I really want my mouth on you."

My fingers began to rub over her clit as my other hand slid under her shirt, moving up to her bra and pulling a cup down so I could get my hands on bare skin. Her nipple hardened almost immediately as my fingers closed around it. She rested her forehead against the door, her breath coming in harsh pants as I drove her body towards climax. As much as I wanted to take my time with her, show her just how high I could take her, I knew this had to be fast, and there was something to be said for a quickie.

"You're so hot and wet." I traced the shell of her ear with the tip of my tongue and she shuddered. "So wet for me."

My cock rubbed against her jeans, the friction almost painful against my sensitive skin. I gave her nipple a sharp tug and she made a strangled sound, like she was trying to hold back.

"That's good," I murmured. "Don't be loud. Wouldn't want someone to come in here and see you about to come on my fingers. And that's what's going to happen, isn't it?"

She nodded, every muscle in her body tense. She

was close. I could feel it.

I nipped at her earlobe and moved my fingers harder and faster, pushing her. She began to tremble and then came with a cry.

"That's it." I kissed the side of her neck, wishing I could mark her flawless skin as she shook in my arms. I kept my fingers moving slowly over her clit, coaxing out every last bit of pleasure I could. When I stilled, I kept my arms around her, my hand on her breast, until I was sure she could stand on her own.

She turned towards me, clothes still in disarray, her eyes shining. She reached out and took the hand that had been in her pants, raising it to her mouth. When she slid my fingers into her mouth, my stomach tightened. Her tongue moved over my skin, thoroughly cleaning each digit. My cock twitched and I knew if she kept it up, I'd be hard again in no time.

I pulled my hand away and leaned down to kiss her, tasting us both in her mouth. Her body pressed against mine and I wondered if there was any way I could get her in bed again before her day of fun was over. I didn't know why I wanted her so badly, and I wasn't going to take the time to try to figure things out. All I knew was we were both here and I was going to give her a day of freedom for her to remember.

Chapter 13

Reed

What happened in the storage room hadn't lessened my desire for her. If anything, it had made it stronger. As we made our way through the city, I found myself constantly wanting to touch her. My arm around her shoulders, at her waist. Hand on the small of her back. Fingers laced between mine.

I barely registered the beauty of Venice even as our gondolier took us on a tour. All of my attention was on Nami and her reaction to everything. She was delighted at the architecture, amused by the other tourists. She was the strangest combination of maturity with child-like joy.

As we went, we also talked and I was again surprised at how easy it was to open up to her. By mid-day, I was telling her things I hadn't discussed with anyone.

"My parents decided that I needed to marry the

daughter of this business partner of theirs. Britni."

A shadow crossed her face, but was gone again before I could really be sure that I'd seen it. "Did you love her?" she asked.

I shook my head. "I barely knew her. She was a few years younger than me. I knew her brother was an ass, so that didn't make me more inclined to like the idea, but it was for my family." I looked down at my left hand where I'd worn a gold band for the short time I'd been married. "I'd been okay with it until I met this girl. Piper. She was in my sister's class."

"The spoiled one?" Nami was smiling, but her eyes were guarded.

I nodded. "I screwed up everything. I thought I was in love with Piper, but I didn't think I could break off the engagement with Britni, so I went through with it."

"You're married?" Nami stiffened and started to pull away from me.

"No," I said quickly. I kept my arm around her, but didn't try to pull her closer, not wanting to be aggressive. "I did marry Britni, but it was the marriage and Piper that finally made me see how miserable I was." This was the first time I'd said all this out loud, I realized.

"What did you do?"

"Well, after I admitted it to myself, I knew I had to do something about it, but I wasn't sure what." I twisted one of Nami's curls around my finger. "Then my brother-in-law did something awful and when I saw how his family rallied around him, I knew I couldn't be a part of it anymore. I filed for divorce."

"And Piper?"

The words were flat and I looked down at Nami, wondering if I could read her thoughts on her face. I couldn't. I supposed I could've lied to her and told her that my divorce was the reason I'd come to Europe, but I didn't want to spoil what we had with a lie. Lies were what had gotten me into trouble in the first place.

"I went to her, told her about the divorce, but it was too late." It didn't hurt to think about it anymore, which is what made me realize I hadn't been in love with Piper after all. "She'd found someone else."

"I'm sorry," Nami said, her voice sincere.

"I'm not," I replied honestly. "She told me that the two of us had been drawn together because of circumstances, nothing else. We really weren't a good match."

"Is she why you came to Europe?"

"Part of it." I shifted in my seat and Nami moved with me, tucking her head against my shoulder. "My parents were furious about the divorce and threatened my job. That's when I realized I couldn't take it anymore. I was tired of doing everything they told me to do."

"And did they accept your decisions?"

I heard the careful tone in her voice and knew we weren't just talking about me anymore. "Not exactly. I quit my job and left. That was a couple months ago."

"And you haven't been back since?"

"No." My fingers traced patterns on Nami's arm. "But I've talked to them a few times."

"And are they okay with your choices now?"

"Not really," I admitted. "But I don't regret doing it. Quitting or divorcing Britni. I've spent too much of my life doing as I was told. It was fine when I was a kid, but I'm far too old to be toeing the line like they wanted me to. I need to choose my own path. Work, love, family. They have to be my choices."

Silence fell over us as our tour guide pulled us up to a spot where we could get off. I helped Nami out of the gondola and she put her arm around my waist, leaning her head against me. I was surprised, but wasn't about to complain. I put my arm around her shoulders and we headed for the *Palácio rosado*.

"It's so beautiful," Nami said softly as we made our way inside.

She was right. The outside had been impressive enough, but the interior with its ornate high ceilings and breath-taking architecture, was spectacular. The tour guide was talking but I didn't hear a word he said and I didn't think Nami did either. She seemed to be deep in thought and I didn't want to interrupt her. Neither of us spoke through the entire tour, but as we broke off at the end and started to walk about on our own, she broke the silence.

"My family has planned my life out." She was staring straight ahead and her voice was soft. I almost thought she might be talking to herself rather than me. "I told you that I majored in political science because it was what they wanted, but it's beyond that. I, too, am supposed to take over my family's...business."

We stood at the Bridge of Sighs, oblivious to everyone else around us. I didn't know what was going on with Nami, but she was clearly dealing with some difficult choices.

"It's been in my family for generations," she continued. "A legacy passed down to the eldest child, boy or girl, and we're expected to rise to it. We're trained for it from birth." There was a hint of bitterness in her voice.

"And what if you refuse?" I asked.

"I can't." She sighed and straightened, pulling away from me. "If my brother had lived, maybe I could have, but he died when he was only a few hours old."

"I'm so sorry," I said.

"I don't remember him," she said absently. "I remember when my mother miscarried though. Twice. How sad everyone was. My parents weren't going to try for another one. Halea was their miracle baby. Four weeks early and so tiny. Even when she finally came home, she was so small I was afraid to hold her."

I had the sudden, sharp memory of my mother handing me a squalling, red-faced bundle. Rebecca had been a handful from moment one, but I'd loved her then. I supposed I still loved her, but I didn't like her very much. I felt a stab of jealousy for what Nami and her sister had. Her parents might've been similar to mine, but she at least had Halea.

"You see, if I choose to step down from my position, it would go to Halea." Nami crossed her arms, rubbing them with her hands as we followed a group of people to see the dungeon. "And she couldn't handle it."

"Does she want it?" I asked. "I know you said she's sixteen, but some people know what they want to do when they're that age."

Nami shook her head. "It doesn't matter. She doesn't have the strength to do it, to deal with everything."

I wondered what sort of business the Carrs owned, but I didn't ask. I was getting the distinct impression that she would only offer the personal details she wanted, and nothing more.

"She wants to please people," Nami continued. "She hates conflict. Always the peacemaker."

I could see where that would be a problem in the business world. While compromise and negotiation always required a bit of flexibility, someone who always wanted to make peace would certainly get walked all over. To be good at being in charge, a person had to have the right combination of stubbornness and a willingness to consider others' opinions.

"There's no one else," she said.

I hated the tone of defeat in her voice. A wave of protectiveness washed over me, surprising me. I'd never been protective of anyone. Not really. I considered myself a gentleman and tried to look out for people, but it was never anything like this. I wanted to hold her and tell her that it would all be okay.

"Can't your parents just hire someone? I know it's not ideal for a family business, but surely there's someone who's been loyal enough to be considered family without being blood."

The smile she gave me said it all. "No, Reed. It has to be me. And I've made my peace with that. More or less, anyway." She reached over and grabbed my hand, squeezing it tightly. "That's why this means so much to me. When I go back, it's all responsibility."

I didn't say anything as I pulled her to my side, tucking her under my arm where she fit so perfectly. I hated this. I hated not being able to help her break free like I had. I hated her parents for making her feel so trapped. And I hated how much I cared. I didn't know this girl. She was supposed to have been a fling, another in a line of hook-ups to help me forget the mess I'd left in Philadelphia and to distract me from the fact that I had no idea what I was doing. But it was more than that already, had been from the moment I'd met her even if I hadn't wanted to admit it then.

I told myself that I needed to stop asking questions, stop trying to figure out a way to help. I couldn't help. All I could do was listen and then let her go when it was time. But as I looked down at her, my heart twisted at the thought of letting her go, never seeing her again.

Dammit. I knew better than to do this, but I couldn't seem to stop myself. I didn't know who she was or what I was feeling, only that it was more than I should. I also knew that no matter what I did, things were going to end badly. For both of us.

Chapter 14

Reed

As afternoon turned into evening, I started getting hungry. With all the craziness that had been going on, I'd forgotten to eat today. I doubted Nami had eaten much either, so I steered us towards a place I'd heard of when I'd been here before. I hadn't eaten there, but it sounded like a good place to take her. I'd heard it had an amazing view of the gondolas. Nice and romantic...

I pushed the thought aside. Romance didn't matter. I wasn't trying to date her. I kept telling myself that as we walked up to Risorrante da Raffaele. Still, I couldn't help but think about what it would be like to take her someplace like this on a real date, as something more than just some girl I'd hooked up with. A girl I was just supposed to be showing a good time.

I could see how things would play out differently

if we'd been here as a couple. We would've been planning the trip together, with the restaurant as part of it. I pulled out her chair for her, returning the smile she gave me. After we ordered, I decided to ask the question I'd been wondering for a while now.

"What would you do," I asked, "if you could do anything? If your family business wasn't a factor. What would you do?"

Nami looked surprised and I understood why. When a person was raised, groomed, to take over the family business, there was never anyone asking what we wanted to do, not seriously anyway. Our opinions, our wants, they didn't matter.

"I haven't given it any thought."

The reply came automatically. I recognized the sound of something that had been rehearsed, the kind of response a responsible older child was supposed to give when asked that question.

"Yes, you have." I called her on her lie. "I know you have because I always did."

She smiled, unapologetic about the deceit. "You did?"

"Of course." I smiled back. "I did the whole MBA thing and found out I have a knack for it, so my dreams changed, but they weren't always for business."

"What were they?" she asked. "When you were a child, what were your dreams?"

"If I tell you mine, will you tell me yours?" I teased as the waiter poured us both the wine I'd ordered.

She winked. "You first."

"All right," I agreed. I leaned back in my chair. "How far back do you want to go? Preschool?"

"You were ambitious even then?" She seemed amused. "Why does this not surprise me?"

"Oh, nothing so ambitious," I said. "I once wanted to be a police car. Not a policeman, but a car."

She laughed, a full, real laugh, not the kind that someone gave to be polite. "You wanted to be a car?"

I shrugged. "I was four. I didn't know that wasn't exactly an option." I took another swallow of wine. "I figured it out eventually."

"So did you want to be a police officer then?"

"No." I shook my head. "When I was older, but before I really understood what it meant for me to take over the family business, I thought I might want to be a lawyer. Not a prosecutor or some sleazy defense attorney. I wanted to go into family law, take care of kids."

It was funny how I thought of that now. I hadn't

thought of it in years, not since I'd gotten into high school and my parents had started telling me what classes to take. Or, as they put it, 'strongly advising' me what would be needed for me to get into business. I'd been surprised that I'd felt protective of Nami, thinking that I hadn't felt that way before, but I had. I'd wanted to help people.

"You're quiet," Nami said, breaking into my thoughts.

"Just remembering," I said. "So there you have it. I wanted to be a lawyer and then went to business school."

"Is that what you will do now?" she asked. "Go to law school?"

I shook my head. "No, I've given that up. I don't think I'd be suited for law anyway. I actually do have a good head for business."

"So you will go back to your parents' business?" She sounded surprised.

"No." I leaned back as the waiter brought our appetizers. "I want my own business." I frowned. "I thought I had a good idea before, but now I'm thinking I might want something else."

"What?" she asked.

"I have no idea." I laughed. "None at all."

We ate for a few moments, enjoying the weather

and the city itself. I had to admit, I was definitely enjoying this trip to Venice much more than my previous one. I looked across the table at Nami. There was no denying that it was due to the company.

"You never told me yours," I said as the waiter cleared away our appetizers and placed our entrees in front of us. "If family wasn't an issue, what would you want to be? What would you do?"

She flushed, piquing my curiosity. Whatever it was, it had to be interesting.

"Now you have to share," I said.

She pushed some of her food around on her plate and took a bite. I didn't press her again. She'd tell me when she was ready. I could see that she wanted to. After a couple minutes of us eating in silence, she finally spoke.

"I wanted to be a teacher."

"A teacher?" I was surprised, not because I didn't think she'd be good at it, but because it didn't seem to match her initial reaction.

"And a mother." She looked down at her plate.

Ah, that made sense now. Well, sort of. "Will your family's business keep you from being a mother?" The question popped out before I thought about it. "Shit. I'm sorry. That's none of my business."

"It's okay," she said, her voice quiet. "Let's just say that if I have children, because of my position, I'd most likely see very little of them. They'd be raised by nannies. Governesses."

"Couldn't your husband take care of them? If you've got such a good position, he wouldn't need to work long hours." Dammit. I kept putting my foot in my mouth, but I couldn't help it. I wanted to know more about her, how she thought, what she wanted. "That is, if you planned to get married. You wouldn't need to just to have kids. I mean, I just assumed since your family was so adamant about the whole sex thing..."

Shit. I sounded like such an idiot. Fortunately, Nami was laughing. It wasn't the same full laugh she'd had before, but it was real.

"Yes, Reed, I would need to be married." She was smiling, but it didn't reach her eyes. "My parents would not approve of children any other way."

I frowned as I took another bite.

"You do not approve." Her accent had thickened and I knew she was upset.

"Actually, I was just thinking of how well our parents would get along." That was half the truth anyway. "My parents put an 'heir' clause in the business contract they drew up when Britni and I got married." I stabbed a piece of chicken with a little more force than necessary. "Kids are just pawns to my parents."

Nami reached across the table and put her hand on mine. I jerked my head up, startled as much by the gesture as I was by the touch itself.

"All we can hope for, then, is to do better for our children than our parents have done for us."

There was something in her voice that made me turn over my hand and squeeze hers, offering her comfort for whatever she was feeling. I raised our hands and kissed the back of hers.

"I'm sure you're going to be a great mother," I said sincerely. I felt a stab of jealousy at the thought of her with another man and immediately shoved it away. I had no right to be jealous. She wasn't mine. This was just a fun follow up to a great night.

"I don't think so." She pulled her hand away from mine. "My eldest will be forced to do exactly what I'm doing now."

I frowned. "But you don't have to do things the same way your parents do. You can let your kids do whatever they want."

She shook her head, but didn't expound. She

went back to eating and silence fell between us again. When the waiter came back to ask if we wanted dessert, we both declined and I asked for the check.

"I'll pay," she said, reaching for her purse.

"No way." I picked up the check and handed the waiter my card. "My treat."

As the waiter walked away, Nami leaned across the table, her expression serious. "Reed, you do understand, this is not a date. It cannot be a date."

"I know," I said. And I did, intellectually. A part of me, however, still had a bit of hope that this could be something more. I didn't know what, because I wasn't letting myself think that far ahead, but something.

She shook her head. "No, you don't. You have to understand that I will have to walk away soon, and we will never see each other again."

I couldn't let her see how much I hated that idea. I stood and held out my hand. "Soon, but not now, right?"

I saw the emotions flit across her face but didn't say anything. She had to make this decision on her own. If she declined and said she needed to go now, I'd respect it. I'd take her wherever she thought it best to find her bodyguards and then I'd go find a hotel room. But I didn't want her to say no. I wanted her to take my hand and come with me somewhere we could be alone. Really alone.

She stood but didn't take my hand. I tried to hide my disappointment as I lowered my hand. This was it then. We were done. I barely registered the waiter returning my card. All I could think about was the best way to say good-bye. I wanted to kiss her one last time, feel her pressed against me.

"Soon." Her voice was low as she closed the distance between us. "But not now."

She stood on her toes and claimed my mouth in a kiss that went straight down through me. I could feel the want, the need, as her tongue curled around mine, her body moving against me in a way that wasn't entirely appropriate for public. I didn't care about anyone who might be watching though. All I cared about was the woman in my arms.

When she broke the kiss, she didn't pull away. "Take me somewhere we can be alone," she whispered.

"You read my mind." I brushed my lips across hers. "Let's get out of here."

Chapter 15

Nami

I didn't know what I expected, but it wasn't something like Hotel Moresco. It was absolutely gorgeous, and far too expensive for a few hours. I had no doubt that was all we would get. Tomas and Kai hadn't caught up with us yet, but I had no doubt that they'd find me soon. Even if they didn't, I would need to call them and meet. I'd missed the plane today, and we could make excuses for that, but if I put off going home for more than a day, I risked my parents finding out what I was really doing.

I should have left him at the restaurant, I knew that, but I hadn't been able to make myself walk away. I'd seen the look in his eyes when I hadn't taken his hand and it had reached something deep inside me, a part of me I hadn't known I'd had. All his talk of dreams and what I wanted had stirred up feelings I hadn't allowed myself to feel in a long time. I'd accepted my parents' will and resigned myself to my position, to marrying a man I didn't know or love. What I'd told him about children was true. I may have been inheriting the title of queen and the rule of Saja, but I was still expected to provide an heir. At least, unlike European monarchies, the gender wasn't important.

It had been that thought, that this was what I'd be doing to my own son or daughter, that had made me go with him. I needed to forget about what was to come, live in the moment, focus on nothing but him. I knew I'd gotten in too deep with him, cared too much, and it was that knowledge that would keep me sane during what was to come. It would be Reed's voice I would hear, his body I would see and feel when my husband came to me.

I'd heard a story once that a young English princess, when she told her mother that she was frightened shortly before her wedding night, was given the sage advice to close her eyes and think of England. I would not be thinking of Saja on my wedding night, gritting my teeth and getting through it. Instead, I would think of Reed. Imagine it was his hands on me, him inside me. My husband would never know that any sounds of pleasure I made were from the memory of the man currently at my side.

"Are you sure about this, Nami?" Reed asked. "I don't want you to do anything you don't want."

I squeezed his hand and led him onto the elevator. "I want you."

His eyes darkened as the doors closed and he backed me up against the wall. He cupped my face between his hands, and I waited for a hard, demanding kiss. I could feel the desire radiating off of him. Instead, his touch was gentle, his thumbs brushing along my bottom lip.

"The things you do to me," he murmured. He lowered his head and touched his lips to mine, the briefest of kisses, but enough to heat my entire body from head to toe.

The elevator dinged and we were on the fourth floor. Reed had gone for whatever room they had available, but I had no doubt that even the cheapest room here would be opulent. I wasn't disappointed, but I only cared about one thing.

I pulled him after me, the bed my only objective.

"Not that I'm complaining," Reed said as I pushed against his chest so that he fell back on the bed. "But I was thinking we could take our time."

"I intend to," I said as I stripped of my shirt and jeans. "I am going to take my time with you."

His eyes widened slightly. "Nami?"

149

I didn't speak as I pulled off his shoes before climbing onto the bed. I straddled his waist and took hold of his t-shirt. He raised up enough for me to pull it off, baring his sculpted, lean torso. I felt his eyes on me as I slowly ran my hands over his chest, down his arms and then back up before moving down to his stomach. I didn't look at him as I teased along the waistband of his jeans, memorizing the way the pants hung low enough to show off the top of those v-grooves that I knew pointed the way to a magnificent piece of flesh.

I leaned down, running my tongue over his abs, enjoying the moans my attention elicited. I traveled up his chest, kissing and licking my way across his skin. When I reached his nipples, I took my time on each one, licking and sucking until he had a hand on my head, fingers buried in my curls. Pinpricks of pain went through my scalp, making things low inside me heat up. I scraped my teeth across the tight skin and he swore. I smiled and bit down, worrying at his nipple until he was writhing beneath me, the friction doing wonderful things to me.

Suddenly, he was pulling me up and crushing my mouth to his. He bit at my bottom lip, sucking it into his mouth to soothe away the sting. His free hand pressed against the small of my back, pushing me even harder down against him, the only thing between us was my panties and his clothing.

"Could I make you come this way?" He paused in his assault on my mouth only long enough to ask the question.

I didn't need to answer because I was already coming. The pressure and friction from his jeans on my clit pushed me over the edge. I pulled my mouth away from his to cry out.

"I love those sounds you make." He sucked on my earlobe and I squirmed, sending new ripples of pleasure through me. "Want to see what else I can make you do?"

I pushed myself up on my knees. "Not yet. I'm not done with you."

He slid his hands up my sides. "Please. You're killing me."

"Maybe a peek." I smiled down at him as I reached behind my back and unhooked my bra.

"Fuck," he groaned as he cupped my breasts. "You have the most amazing tits."

My eyelids fluttered as his fingers found my nipples, rolling them hard and fast, almost painfully. He tugged on them and my head fell back, my body arching towards his touch. I put my hands on his chest, feeling the rise and fall against my palms, the beat of his heart.

His hips moved under mine and I felt his weight starting to shift. I shook my head and slid backwards, moving away from his hands.

"I'm not done with you yet." I positioned myself at his knees and got to work ridding him of his jeans. I left his boxer-briefs on, wanting to remember the sight of him like this. Long legs, trim waist. The way the cloth clung to him. His cock was already starting to grow and I licked my lips in appreciation, remembering the taste of him from earlier today.

I ran my hands up his muscular legs, the hair rough against my palms. I cupped his cock through the cloth and gave him a gentle squeeze, smiling as he swore. I hooked my fingers under the waistband of his underwear and he obliged by lifting his hips so I could pull them down and then off. His cock came free, thick and swollen. I sat back on my heels, letting myself enjoy the new view.

"You going to stare at it all night or do something with it?" He was teasing, but I could hear the strain in his voice.

I didn't answer him, but instead reached out and lightly ran my fingers along the underside of his cock. It twitched and his hands fisted in the bedspread. He swore and begged, but I didn't let him hurry me. I let my fingers explore every inch of his shaft, never giving him enough pressure. When I was done with that, I moved lower, cupping his balls, rolling them between my fingers, feeling the weight of them, the soft skin holding them.

"Please, Nami, I'm dying here."

I smiled. My panties were soaked, my pussy throbbing. I was as desperate for him as he was for me. I shifted, pulling off my panties and tossing them on the floor. I started to rise on my knees, then hesitated. There was something I wanted, but I wasn't sure how to ask it.

"What is it?"

My eyebrows went up. I hadn't thought my face was that easy to read. Or was it just that Reed knew me that well?

"Nami." His hand touched mine as he sat up. "What is it? If you've changed your mind..."

"No," I quickly assured him. "I was just wondering if..." I could feel heat rising to my face, and it wasn't from arousal. "Never mind." I looked away.

"Hey." He hooked a finger under my chin and turned my face back towards him. "Whatever it is, you can ask me."

I wasn't sure if it was the look in his eyes or the

fact that I knew this might be my last chance to have what I wanted, but I managed to force the words out.

"I want to feel you."

"Nami..."

"Only you." I saw him swallow hard. "Nothing between us."

His hand tightened on mine.

"I'm on the pill," I said. "But if there's a reason..."

"No." He shook his head. "I always...I mean, I'm clean."

"It's okay if you don't want to. I know some guys don't trust..."

"I trust you." His words were firm. "Is this what you want?"

I didn't answer right away. I knew it was risky. He said he trusted me, but the trust had to go both ways. I didn't think he was lying to me, so there was that.

I looked straight into his amazing dark eyes. "If you want to..."

His mouth covered mine, silencing the rest of my statement. I let him lay me back on the bed, let him take control. I wanted to feel the weight of him on me, the way his muscles bunched and moved under his skin. His tongue thrust into my mouth even as he entered me with one smooth stroke.

My back arched and I cried out. Painful pleasure went through me with a shock, electricity shooting across my nerves as he opened me. He swallowed every sound as he drove us both towards our release. He stretched me wide around him, rubbing against every bit of me. The base of his cock pressed against my swollen clit and I dug my nails into his shoulders.

His lips began to make a trail down my jaw and I could hear my moans, loud in the relative silence. I should've been embarrassed, but all I could think about was how amazing he made me feel and not caring who knew it. As his mouth traveled down my neck, I made another decision. I was so close and there was one final thing I wanted.

"Mark me."

He froze, raising his head so that our eyes met.

"My breast," I said. "So my parents won't see it."

He gave me a quick, bruising kiss and then buried his face against my breast. I gasped as he teased my nipple with his teeth, a sound that turned into a sharper cry as he began to suck on the skin next to it, drawing it into his mouth even as he kept steady, rhythmic strokes. His fingers raked through my hair, ran down my face, my sides. I was aware of all of it, every place he touched me. I was on fire, racing for a full-on explosion.

"Come, Nami." Reed's voice was ragged and I could feel him start to lose control. "Please, baby, come for me. I'm so close."

There was tenderness in his voice, something more than just lust. That did it, took down the last of what I was holding back. I let go, let him hear me call out his name, and then I felt him shudder, his cock emptying inside me. The warmth filled me, adding to the flames consuming me. I could feel the world starting to gray out, but I fought it back, needing to feel all of it. If this was the last time, I wanted to memorize every sound, scent and sensation. I would never see Reed again, but this would stay with me, warm me, keep me. No matter what happened.

Chapter 16

Reed

I couldn't breathe. My heart was pounding, my blood roaring in my ears. All of that, however, was secondary to her. Every place our bodies touched, my skin hummed. I was more aware of her than I'd ever been of anyone else in my life. I rolled us onto our side without pulling out of her. I wanted to stay as close to her as possible, keep us joined until I had no choice but to let her go.

It was foolish, I knew, to allow myself to get so attached. She'd made it clear that there could never be anything between us, that when she left, I'd never see her again. Drawing this out would only make it that much harder when she had to go. I couldn't help myself though. I'd told her that I wanted her, but that word seemed inadequate to describe what I felt towards her. She was a craving, an addiction. Every moment I spent with her just fed the habit. I couldn't be near her without needing to touch her. Despite that, it wasn't only physical. I wanted to make her smile, protect her from everything and everyone who would hurt her.

"You're thinking." Nami pushed hair back from

my face. "I must not have been very good if you can think so soon after."

I took her face between my hands. "I'm thinking about you. Only you." I kissed her fiercely, trying to put all the things I was feeling into that one action. I couldn't tell her because I didn't understand it myself, but I wanted her to know.

A knock at the door interrupted us and I frowned. I rolled over, reluctantly leaving her warm embrace. I grabbed my pants and pulled them on, grimacing as the jeans chafed my cock. I headed out to the main area as I zipped up.

"Who is it?" I called as the person knocked again.

"Mr. Stirling, it's the hotel manager."

Well that couldn't be good. The only times I'd ever seen a manager come to a room was when someone had done something stupid or trashed it. Since I'd done neither, I had a feeling it could only be one thing. And, I guess, technically, I had done something stupid.

"Reed." Nami's voice was soft behind me. "Is it them?"

I glanced over my shoulder and saw that she had the bed sheet wrapped around her. My stomach tightened at the sight. She was covered, but I knew she wasn't wearing anything under that sheet. Nothing but the mark I'd left on her breast.

"Mr. Stirling, there are two gentlemen out here who wish to speak with you and your lady friend."

I could tell by his tone that he wasn't happy with me. He sounded polite enough, but I'd spent hours in hotels like this and could tell the difference between professionally polite and genuine cordiality, even in heavily accented English. I didn't answer, looking to Nami to see what she wanted to do.

"Let them in," she said. She straightened, shoulders back and chin up. The vulnerability she'd had with me was gone. Whoever her parents had brought her up to be, that's who she was now.

"Just a minute," I said as I turned back towards the door. I took a deep breath and opened the door.

I stepped back so that I was at Nami's side, not touching, but close enough to make it clear she was with me. I knew she'd said that her bodyguards wouldn't hurt her, but I wasn't entirely sure I trusted them. The impression I'd gotten from Nami had been that she'd never really done anything like this before, which meant she couldn't know how they'd react, not really. And I'd be damned if I let anyone lay a finger on her.

The manager came in first, the expression on his

face carefully blank. I had no doubt he'd seen much worse than this. Following him were Tomas and Kai. Even though they didn't really look alike – aside from their bulk – I didn't know which one was which. They weren't wearing blank expressions. They were pissed. I automatically took a step forward and to the side, shielding Nami. I caught a glimpse of surprise on their faces, but it passed quickly.

"It's okay, Reed," Nami said. She put her hand on my arm as she stepped up next to me. "Tomas and Kai won't hurt me."

My hands curled into fists, but I didn't argue with her. I'd let her believe it, but if either one of them came near her, they'd have to go through me first.

"We have spoken with your father." One of the men spoke to her as if I wasn't even there. His voice was surprisingly soft for such a large man. "We told him that we experienced some technical difficulties that delayed our flight." He glared at me. "But we must go. Now."

Nami slid her hand down my arm until she reached my hand. Her fingers threaded between mine. "And if I do not wish to leave right now?"

The other one spoke, his voice apologetic, but

firm. "Then we will involve the police."

"The police?" Nami echoed. "What are you talking about, Kai?"

Kai looked at me, his gaze anything but friendly. "We will tell the police that this American kidnapped you and violated you."

My mouth dropped open. Was he serious?

"You cannot do that." Her hand squeezed mine. "I went with him willingly. I will not support your story."

"You will have no choice." The one who must've been Tomas spoke up. "The media will pick up the story and your only options will be to confess the truth to the world or go along with the lie."

I found my voice. "I don't know who you two think you are, but I'm not some nobody. My family has money and influence too. I'll have the best lawyer in Venice on my side and I won't just refute the charges, I'll file lawsuits against both of you for defamation of character."

The look Kai gave me told me clearly that he thought me beneath him, no matter what I'd just said.

"Can I speak with you for a moment?" I turned my back on the bodyguards and looked down at Nami. "Privately."

She looked at Tomas and Kai. "Give us a moment." When they didn't move, her voice hardened. "Now."

Neither one of them looked happy, but they stepped back into the hallway and closed the door behind them. I had no doubt they'd taken up their post there, ready to do whatever was necessary to get Nami home.

"I'm sorry, Reed," she apologized. "I never thought things would go this far."

I made a dismissive gesture. "You don't have to go with them, Nami. I'll protect you. Let them try to get me arrested. I wasn't kidding when I said I could have the best lawyer in the city. And that's not counting the American lawyers my parents would send as soon as I called home." I took both of her hands. "I'm sure my family knows people here that will make a big enough fuss that nothing will happen to me."

"But they're right," she said. Her smile was sad. "If the press picked up the story, I would have only two choices. One, to hurt you and lie, or two, tell the truth and ruin my family."

My heart gave a painful thud. "Admitting to being with me would ruin your family?"

She raised our hands and kissed my knuckles.

162

"Admitting to what happened between us would. Maybe not ruin, but certainly harm."

"I thought you said your parents weren't that old-fashioned."

"You don't understand."

The words were gentle, but they sparked my temper.

"What do you mean I don't understand? I'm probably the only person who can come close to understanding. I know what it's like to have parents pressuring you to do what they want you to do. Mine forced me into an arranged marriage, for fuck's sake!" My voice was rising and I struggled to keep it down. I wasn't angry with her, not really. I was angry at the circumstances, the stupid little things that were keeping us apart. Her family. Her sense of duty.

"No, Reed." She pulled her hands out of my grasp and took a step back. She took a deep breath, a resigned look on her face. "You don't understand because my parents aren't some rich family with a business they want me to run."

I looked at her, confused. Had she lied to me? Was she trying to scam me? Get money from my family? A thousand possibilities ran through my head, each one worse than the last. Were my

163

instincts with women that awful? Granted, Piper was as good as I'd thought she was, just not the right girl for me. Britni, I'd known she wasn't the kind of woman I wanted. Maybe it wasn't bad instincts, but rather bad luck.

Then Nami said the last thing I expected.

"Reed, I'm a princess."

Chapter 17

Reed

"Excuse me?" I had to have heard her wrong. I could've sworn she'd just said that she was a princess, but that couldn't be right.

Could it?

She spoke stiffly, formally. "I am Princess Nami Carr, eldest child of King Raj and Queen Mara, heir to the throne."

I stared at her. This had to be some sort of joke. A weird, twisted prank.

"Tomas and Kai are my bodyguards, my protectors," she continued. "But they were also sent to the States and Europe with me to make sure I didn't do anything that would embarrass my family...or cause problems with my betrothal."

"Betrothal?" This kept getting better. I was getting light-headed. "You're engaged?" The thought occurred to me that Piper would've appreciated the irony of me falling for someone who was engaged.

"Not officially," she said. "Like you, I was given no choice in the matter. My parents are in the process of selecting an appropriate husband for me. A man from my country who has a good name and a good family."

"And who wants to be king," I quipped, trying to make a joke out of it. This couldn't be happening.

"No." She shook her head. "I will rule. He will be king in name only. Our children will inherit the throne when I am gone. His bloodline will rule only because it is a part of mine." She stopped suddenly and waved a hand dismissively. "That's not important."

I sat down on the arm of the couch, not trusting my legs to hold me. "Right. The succession of monarchs isn't important."

She gave me a sharp look and I could see the hurt in her eyes. I immediately regretted my flippant remark.

"It's just a lot to take in, Nami...I mean, Princess."

"Don't call me that!" she snapped.

Her face was flushed, but I knew it wasn't because of arousal or embarrassment. She was pissed and I was pretty sure it was at me. And I deserved it.

"This is why I did not tell you when we first met." Her eyes were dark and flashing, the color of an ocean during a storm. "I have spent my whole life as Princess Nami, one day to be queen. Never knowing if someone wanted to be close to me for my title, for royal favor. I wanted only to be wanted for me."

Now I really felt like shit. I stood and crossed the distance between us quickly. She didn't move or reach out to me, her jaw set.

"I'm sorry," I apologized. I pushed back a curl from her forehead and let my fingers linger for a moment. "I was shocked and acted like an ass."

She relaxed a bit, but still didn't try to touch me. Her arms hung at her sides, her hands clenched into fists.

"Please, Nami. Forgive me." I went for quiet and sincere rather than charming. I put my hands on her shoulders, but didn't try to pull her towards me. If she came to me, it would be her choice.

Suddenly, her shoulders sagged and she leaned against me, her free arms sliding around my waist as she rested her head on my chest. Her other hand clutched the sheet to her chest. I wrapped my arms around her, closing my eyes as I kissed the top of her head.

"I wanted to tell you," she confessed. "When you were telling me about your family and everything that happened. I wanted to share it all with you, but I didn't want you to look at me differently. I wanted to be seen as just me."

"There's nothing 'just' about you." I looked down at her as she tilted her head back so she could see my face. "And knowing who you are...it makes me admire you more. It took a lot of guts to rebel." I paused, and then tried to lighten the mood by adding, "The whole political science major thing makes a lot more sense now."

That got a faint smile. "Just one small step in the process that started when I was born. Training for the throne. Etiquette and language classes outside of my regular classes. In depth history of most countries. Knowledge of treaties and trade agreements." She sighed.

"And that's why you won't abdicate," I said, understanding. "Why you won't hand things over to your sister. You don't want her to have to go through all of that."

She nodded. "If my brother had lived, I could have turned things over to him and no one would've thought worse of me for it. There are plenty of countries we deal with who have issues with women in power."

"You're right," I said. "Your situation is definitely different than mine. My parents can hire someone to take over the company if Rebecca screws things up. You have an entire country relying on you."

"And that's why this meant so much to me." Her hand slid up and down my bare back as she turned her face and pressed a kiss over my heart. "Time to be me and not have to worry about my responsibilities."

"Because you have to go home and be the crown princess again," I said.

"Right." She flicked her tongue against my nipple and I bit back a moan. "And that means marrying a stranger. Bearing his children and letting another raise them. Even if I'm not queen yet, I won't be allowed to raise them the way a normal person would raise their children."

"And you don't want your husband doing it either." I wasn't sure how I knew it, but I did.

"I don't know him," she said. "What kind of man and father he will be. Maybe he'll be a good man and I will grow to love him."

I tried not to acknowledge the flare of jealousy

that went through me at the thought of her loving another man. Of another man touching her. Making love to her. I clenched my jaw. She wasn't mine, I reminded myself.

"If that is the best I could hope for, I wanted to have something I could remember." Her fingers traced patterns on my lower back. "That's why I slept with my best friend in college, so I would not have my first time be with a stranger."

"And me?" I asked softly.

"You." She made a quiet sound that might have been a sigh. She pulled her arm between us so she could put her hand over my heart.

"I'm a stranger."

She smiled and pressed her lips against my chest, heating my bare skin. "But you wanted me. Not the princess or the chance to see your child on the throne. Me."

"And what was that about?" I asked, gesturing back towards the bedroom with my head. "Taking it slow. Wanting me to..."

I swallowed hard at the memory. I'd never done that before, not even with Britni. Even thought we'd been contractually required to try to start having kids shortly after marriage, I'd kept making excuses about why I wanted to wait just a bit longer. I'd never had sex without a condom.

Nami's face turned red and I thought she'd refuse to answer, but she didn't. I supposed since her big secret was out of the bag, there wasn't any point in hiding anything else.

"I wanted to remember you," she said. "What you feel like, smell like, sound like. When *he* is touching me, I wanted to be able to close my eyes and imagine it was you."

Fuck. My fingers flexed on her waist and I told my rebellious cock that it wasn't allowed to get hard again.

"We will be expected to start a family immediately," she continued. "And I wanted to remember what you felt like inside me, what it felt like to have nothing between us, to have you come inside me. I thought that if I had those memories, perhaps doing my duty would not be as unpleasant."

Yeah, my cock was definitely not listening to me. I closed my eyes and rested my forehead against hers. "I hate this," I admitted. "I hate knowing you'll be forced into a marriage you don't want. Into the bed of a man who won't know how to please you." I didn't add what I was thinking. A man who might hurt her. I pushed the thought away. I couldn't bear to think of someone harming her.

"You had an arranged marriage," she reminded me.

I raised my head and gave her a wry smile. "And you see how well that turned out. But at least I'd had an idea of who Britni was." I ran my fingers through the hair above her ear. "Besides, even though I didn't love her, both of us were willing. What he'll do..." My fingers curled into fists at her sides. "It's almost rape."

She shook her head. "Nothing will happen without my consent. No one will force me."

"Isn't that what your parents are doing?" I asked. "By making you marry this man, they're forcing you to sleep with him."

"I'm agreeing to the marriage," she said, reaching up to put her hand on my cheek. "And I understand everything that goes along with it. It's my choice."

I wanted to ask if *he* was her choice, but I knew I didn't have the right to ask it. She'd told me that we could never be anything more than this, and I'd told myself I was okay with it. After all, I wasn't looking for a relationship. That was the last thing I needed right now. Especially a relationship with a princess.

"I have to go." She started to pull away from me. "I'm sure Tomas and Kai are getting restless. And they will make trouble for you." She reached up and ran her fingers through my hair. "Even if nothing came of it, I'd never forgive myself for causing you such problems."

I couldn't do it. Not yet. "Give me tonight."

She froze, still in my arms.

"One whole night," I continued. My pulse was racing. "Spend one more night with me. You can leave in the morning." I heard the pleading note in my voice but didn't care. I needed to have her one last time.

She looked at me for a moment and stepped out of my embrace. My stomach twisted into knots. She would leave and I would never see her again.

"Tomas. Kai," she called out loud enough for the pair in the hallway to hear her.

They came back in, looking just as pissed off as before.

"Call my father and tell him that we'll be leaving first thing in the morning." She glanced at me, but kept her face expressionless. "I'm spending tonight with Reed."

"Princess, we cannot allow it." Kai's voice was firm.

"You can and you will," she said. There was steel in her voice and I knew that was her queen voice, the

173

one she would use to rule. "You know what will happen if word gets out about what's happened here. And I will make sure my father knows that you both failed in your duty to keep me...pure. More than once."

I couldn't believe she could sound so sure of herself when she was wearing only a sheet, her curls mussed from sex. It was sexy as hell.

"You two will be solely responsible for the dissolution of my engagement. You will be dismissed in disgrace, unable to find employment anywhere. People may talk about me, but you will be the ones who are blamed."

Both men shifted uncomfortably.

"So, you will do as you are told. Call my father. Make preparations to leave tomorrow morning." She paused, and then added, "I give you my word. I will get on that plane tomorrow morning without complaint."

They exchanged looks, then nodded.

"Very good," she said. "Now go."

When the door closed behind them, she turned and looked at me. "One more night."

Chapter 18

Reed

A million things ran through my mind. All the things I wanted to do to her, and I knew I didn't have enough time. For a moment, I wondered if forever would've been enough for me to have my fill of her, but I pushed the thought aside. There was no need to think of things that weren't possible, especially when our time together was short.

Keeping my eyes locked with hers, I reached out and wrapped my fingers around her hand. Her fingers loosened as I pulled her hand back and the sheet covering her dropped to the floor.

"It's my turn to take it slow," I said as I ran my gaze down her body. "And not only because I want to remember every dip and curve, every magnificent inch of you." I took a step towards her. "I'm going to make sure you'll always remember me." I ran the tip of my finger down the slope of her breast. "That you'll never forget me."

"I don't think that is possible." She raised my hand to her mouth and slid my finger between her lips. As she sucked on it, my cock began to harden, remembering what it was like to have that hot suction surrounding me.

As much as I liked what she was doing, I'd meant what I'd said. It was my turn. I gently pulled my hand away and went down on my knees. There was enough of a height difference that I was able to press my lips against her stomach before bending down to taste more interesting parts.

She moaned as I ran my tongue along her folds, the skin still sensitive from what we'd been doing not too long ago. I put one hand at the small of her back to steady her and lifted her leg to hook it over my shoulder, opening her up to me. As I slowly licked every inch of her, her body danced and moved above me. I could taste myself on her, in her, and I savored our combination. I memorized every dip, the texture of her skin against my tongue. When I began to tease her clit, she buried her hands in my hair, my name coming in gasps. She was close and I wrapped my lips around her clit, sucking on it the way she'd sucked on my finger.

She came fast and hard, her hands tightening

painfully in my hair. The keening sound she made sent a stab of pride through me. She'd been so quiet before and I loved that I could break through that. Part of me wondered if her bodyguards could hear her, and not a small part of me wished they could.

"Stop, stop," she begged, pulling my head away from her. "Too much."

I smiled as I eased her leg off of my shoulder and stood. "I'm just getting started." I cupped the back of her head and kissed her. Even in this I took my time, my tongue thoroughly exploring every inch. Her tongue curled around mine, sliding back into my mouth.

I ran my hands down her back, fingers tracing the ridge of her spine as they made their way down to her ass. I cupped the firm muscles and lifted her. She squeaked in surprise, but I swallowed the sound and held her body against mine, my cock brushing against her ass. Her legs wrapped around my waist and I walked us back to the bedroom, not breaking the kiss the entire way.

My knees bumped against the bed and I lowered her to the mattress. Her body stretched out beneath mine, all soft curves and firm muscle. I ran my hands down her sides, over her hips, committing them to memory. My knee was between her legs and she ground down against me as I moved my mouth down her jaw to her throat. I placed open-mouthed kisses along her neck, tasting the salt of sweat, the tang of her skin.

Her body writhed under my touch and I imagined what she must've been feeling. My own skin felt like a live wire, like the slightest touch would set me off. I slid down her body, lips and tongue making a path across her collarbones and down between her breasts. I took them each in hand, memorizing the shape and feel of them, the weight of them. When I covered her nipple with my mouth, she made another of those delightful sounds. I wished I could spend hours seeing just how many different kinds of sounds I could coax from her.

My fingers attended to the nipple not in my mouth, rolling until it was as hard as the one I sucked on. I alternated my tongue and lips, teasing and suction, storing away every noise for the future. A future without her.

I put that aside. She was here, now, her body hot and needy beneath mine. That was all that mattered. I moved to the other breast, paying equal attention to it before moving further down her body. I ran the tip of my tongue down her stomach, pausing to tease her bellybutton until she squirmed.

When I settled between her legs, I looked up at her. "I'm going to make you come again." She took a shuddering breath. "One more time before I take you." I kissed the inside of her thigh. "And I want to hear you scream my name."

I didn't wait for her to respond. I put my mouth on her thigh again, pulling the skin into my mouth, worrying at it until I left a dark mark on her dusky skin. She'd told me I couldn't mark anywhere her parents would see. Unless she married when she stepped off the plane or decided to go swimming, no one would see this.

When I was satisfied, I turned my attention elsewhere. I knew her clit had to be sensitive, so I avoided it, circling her entrance with my finger before sliding it inside. She said something that I was pretty sure wasn't English, but it didn't sound like she wanted me to stop. I kept my strokes slow, easing her into another orgasm. I knew if I moved too hard, too fast, it would hurt and not in a good way.

Only when she stopped talking and started moaning did I add a second finger. Her body stretched to accommodate the digits and I worked them slowly before curling my fingers to press against that spot inside her. Her entire body jerked and I knew I'd found it again. I took a moment to marvel at how well I knew her body after just a short time together, and then I returned to worshiping it.

"Come on, baby." I brushed my thumb across the top of her clit even as I rubbed her g-spot. "Come for me."

"Yes!" Her back arched and her hips jerked, pushing my fingers deeper.

I nipped at the soft skin of her thigh and her body tensed, pussy gripping my fingers. I hissed, remembering what it had felt like to feel her tightening around my cock like that. I managed to move enough to keep pressure on that spot, driving her higher until she was pleading for me to stop.

I withdrew my hand and pushed myself back on my knees. My cock was hard, pressing painfully against my zipper. I almost wished I'd put my underwear back on when I'd gotten out of bed. I climbed off the bed, not taking my eyes off of her body even as I stripped off my jeans. She was glistening with sweat, her skin shining. Her body still quivered, her eyes wide and dark. I wanted to see her like this whenever I closed my eyes. She was the most beautiful thing I'd ever seen.

I wrapped my hand around the base of my cock, holding it tight. I needed as much time to regain my own composure as she did. Every fiber of my being was begging me to bury myself inside her, take her hard and fast, find my own release inside her. I wasn't going to do it though. This was our last night together, the last chance I had to make sure she remembered me. I wanted her to think of me when that other man kissed her, touched her. I wanted it to be my name she had to force back when she came.

"Reed." She held up a shaking hand.

I climbed onto the bed and knelt between her legs. I took her hand, brushing my lips across her knuckles before releasing it. I leaned forward, cradling her neck, tipping her head to give me easier access to her mouth. I took a long, deep drink of her, then moved back so I could watch her face as I slid home.

"Ahh." The long, drawn out sigh passed between her lips as I took her in one steady thrust. Her eyes were glazed, her body rising to meet mine.

I rested my weight on my elbows, keeping enough space between our bodies so that I wasn't crushing her, but I could still feel her skin slide against mine. I kept my strokes slow and steady, withdrawing almost the whole way before filling her again. Neither of us spoke as our bodies moved together. Without her saying it, I knew she was doing the same thing I was, committing each movement to memory. Registering every nuance, every sensation.

She raised her hand, tracing my face with her fingertips. My cheekbone across to my nose. My jaw and then over my lips. I darted my tongue out to lick the pad of her finger.

"I will never forget you," she whispered.

My heart clenched painfully in my chest. There was too much emotion in those words, too much for how little we knew each other, but I felt it too and it was my undoing. My body tensed as I began to come, but I thrust into her again, needing her to come with me, needing to feel her come apart. Her body jerked as the base of my cock rubbed against her clit and she stiffened.

"Let go." I scraped my teeth against her neck and that was it.

"Reed!"

It wasn't quite a scream, but it was my name and it was enough. I squeezed my eyes closed and pressed my face against her neck. She would remember me and I would remember her. We would never be more than this, but we wouldn't forget either. It would be enough. It had to be.

Chapter 19

Nami

I told him I wouldn't forget him and it was true. But probably not a wise thing to say. It was too much, too soon, but we wouldn't have anything else. I couldn't wait for a future moment because we didn't have one. This was it. He hadn't said it back to me, but I'd seen the look in his eyes when I'd said it. It had been enough.

It had taken all of my self-control not to succumb to the tears welling up in my eyes as Reed and I came. The finality of the moment hit me and I was thankful Reed wasn't looking at me. By the time he raised his head, I'd gotten my emotions under control.

He rolled us over and, as he slipped out of me, I felt a pang of loss. I wondered if it would feel the same when I slept with my husband. Would I wish he was still inside me or would I be grateful that he was done? Reed pulled me back against him, wrapping his body around mine. I snuggled back against him, grateful that I had asked for the whole night.

"Are you okay?" Reed asked, his voice low.

I nodded, not trusting my voice to speak.

"Get some sleep." He kissed my temple. "I'll be here when you wake up."

I pulled his arms more tightly around me. I didn't think I could to sleep, but I had no problem lying here in his arms while he slept. I'd never shared a bed with someone, not even by accident. Tomas and Kai had been diligent about me never falling asleep when Aaron and I hung out. The night we'd slept together, I'd left almost immediately after it was over.

Now, with Reed's arms around me, I knew what I'd been missing. Warmth. Safety. I felt his heart beating against my back, the slow rise and fall of his chest. The faint stubble on his cheeks was rough as he tucked his chin against me. I could feel his cock against my ass, soft and still slick with the results of our union. The logical part of me said we should clean up, but I was content where I was and didn't want to go anywhere.

The last thought was sleepy and I was surprised to feel my eyelids starting to fall. I'd rest them, I decided. It wasn't like I could see Reed anyway. It was more about feeling him. I was still concentrating on the various places our bodies touched when I finally slipped under.

I didn't know how long I slept, only that morning light was peeking between the curtains. It was still early though and, like he'd promised, Reed was still there. He'd shifted at some point during the night. We both had. He was on his back and I was laying half on his chest, one of his arms wrapped around me, his other hand on his stomach. The sheet was low on his waist, barely hiding what I knew was underneath.

I looked up at him, enjoying the chance to see him in a new way. He looked much younger asleep, closer to my age than to thirty. His face was relaxed, with none of the worry I'd seen. Even when he'd been laughing or we'd been in bed, there had still been little lines on his face. Based on what he'd told me about the stress he'd been under back in the States, I supposed it wasn't surprising. Now, however, all of that was gone.

I shifted slowly, not wanting to wake him, but needing to see him better. His hand slid down my back, coming to rest just above my ass, but he didn't wake up. I reached out, hesitating with my hand just above his face. I traced his lips with the lightest of touches, letting my fingers memorize their shape and feel. I could feel them now, the ghost of them on my mouth, between my legs, on my body.

Heat pooled in my stomach. I wanted him again. I wished I had more time. That I could take him in my mouth while he was still soft, feel him grow and swell as I licked and sucked the soft flesh. I hadn't gone down on Aaron that night. Reed was the only man I'd taken in my mouth and the memory of his taste was still thick on my tongue.

Before Reed, I'd never imagined I'd want to do something like that, but I'd loved the sounds he'd made, the way I felt. I loved that I could make him come apart, the look in his eyes when I'd swallowed every drop. I hadn't known what I was doing, but I didn't doubt I'd done well.

I was surprised at how easily sex had come to me. Things had been awkward with Aaron, but he'd assured me that first times were always like that. I wasn't sure that the difference between the first and second time was that drastic with everyone, but there hadn't been any awkwardness with Reed. It had felt natural, right. My body had moved with his in a way it hadn't with Aaron, and I didn't think it was simply because I'd done it once before.

His hair fell across his forehead and I gently pushed it back. I smiled at the mess it was. I could almost imagine him struggling with it before going in to work, trying to get it to lie flat. I wondered if it ever did, but as much as I tried, I couldn't quite picture him with neatly combed hair. In a suit, yes, but not looking like the hundreds of other businessmen I'd seen. My smile widened. It didn't matter what he wore or how he looked. Reed could never be like anyone else.

A lump rose in my throat and my eyes pricked with tears. I couldn't put it off any longer. I eased out from under his arm. I'd promised Tomas and Kai that I would leave with them, and I meant to keep my word. I wouldn't give them any excuse to burst back in. Reed and I'd had our perfect night together and I would keep that memory safe, untainted by a confrontation.

I climbed off of the bed as carefully as I could. I didn't want to say good-bye. Mostly because I didn't know how to do it. We'd already done the awkward one-night stand good-bye, but this time it was different. He meant more to me than just a single night. But I didn't know what that actually meant. I couldn't tell him that I hoped we'd see each other again, because that could never happen. If he woke up, I wouldn't know what to say.

And I couldn't say for certain that I'd have the strength to leave him if he did. One kiss, even a kiss good-bye, and I couldn't guarantee I'd be able to walk away. I didn't think clearly when I was with him, when he was touching me. The very fact that I was here was evidence to that. Before I'd met him, my rebellions had been little ones. I would never have dreamed of spending a day in Venice without my bodyguards, but he emboldened me, made me act more impulsively than I ever had before. Even my rebellions had been planned out.

I gathered up my clothes from where I'd left them and headed into the bathroom. I didn't take a shower, not wanting to waste the time or risk Reed waking. I cleaned up as quickly and as best I could, then dressed again. I scowled as I pulled on the clothes I'd worn yesterday. I hated the feel of them, but I didn't have any other options. At least one good thing would come out of having to go straight to the plane and home. No one would think it weird I wanted to shower, put on some clean clothes and sleep.

How different this would be if I'd just been some girl he'd met in Paris. Someone with a normal family.

I shook my head and splashed cold water on my face. I couldn't think of that now. The time for flights of fancy and daydreams had passed. It was time to move on, to do my duty. I knew what it would mean and what was expected of me. I'd been raised for this. Born for this.

I took a steadying breath and walked back into the bedroom. I'd half expected Reed to be awake, but he was where I'd left him. More or less. He was on his side now, but he still appeared to be asleep. That was good. I didn't want him awake, but I also didn't want to leave without something to say good-bye. Reed deserved better than that.

On the desk was a sheaf of paper and a pen. A note would have to do. I stood there for a moment, wondering what to write. The words came more easily than I'd thought and it didn't take me long to get them all down. I folded the note and turned towards the bed. I set it on the end table and let myself have one final look at Reed. I leaned down and brushed my lips across his forehead. I couldn't stop the tear that trailed down my cheek, but I hurried out of the room before others could follow.

I'd wanted the time with Reed so I'd always remember him, but as I left the bedroom, I knew I couldn't hope for Reed to do the same. He needed to forget me. And that's what I'd told him.

My note had been simple.

Thank you for giving me what I needed. I can move on with my life now. I wish you all the happiness in the world.

And I did wish him that. I just wished that he could've been happy with me.

Chapter 20

Reed

I hadn't fallen asleep with any of the women I'd slept with since leaving the States, but it had felt natural to do so with Nami. Her body fit perfectly against mine, back against my chest, head tucked under my chin. I'd wanted to stay awake all night, knowing that I wouldn't have this chance again, but the lack of sleep the previous night and a busy day were a strong combination and I hadn't been able to resist. It was a deep, dreamless sleep and when I started to gradually wake it was that slow, thick waking, the kind that felt like swimming through molasses.

The first thing I knew was that she was no longer in bed with me. Her body heat was gone, but I could hear her moving around. I kept my eyes closed until I heard a door close. I opened my eyes and saw that she'd gone into the bathroom. I rolled onto my side, unsure of what I should do.

Would it be better to let her know I was up? Should I actually get up and dress so I could walk her to the door? Or would it be better to stay in the bed and say good-bye from here? That felt crass. But what would I say when she walked out of the bathroom? A simple 'good morning' felt trite, but I didn't think it'd be fair to expect anything else.

I didn't know how to do this. How to say good-bye. The other women I'd slept with had either left when we were done, or I'd been the one leaving. There hadn't been cuddling, sleeping, lingering. There'd been no expectations and no hard feelings. Before everything had gone to hell back home, I'd dated, but in those instances, the morning after good-byes hadn't been weird because I'd known I'd be seeing them again. With Nami, that wasn't the case. I had no clue what was appropriate.

I had another problem with not knowing what to say. It was less about appropriate and more about not being able to find the right words to either tell her what I felt or to hide it. Would it be fair to tell her that I didn't want her to go? Would she think it was a ploy, just me saying it to make what we'd done feel less like a hook-up?

And if she believed I was telling the truth, what

then? It wouldn't change anything. Before she'd told me the truth, I might've thought she could do what I'd done and break away, but I knew now that wasn't a possibility. A family business was one thing. A kingdom was another. And telling her that I wanted to see her again would just be cruel to both of us. We both knew it wasn't going to happen.

The other option was just as unappealing. If I walked her to the door or stayed in bed, only telling her good-bye and that it had been fun, would she think I didn't care? Would she believe this entire thing had only a mere blip on my radar? Her words to me echoed in my mind. She said she would never forget me. I felt the same way. No matter where I went from here, I'd never forget her and the short time we had together.

I was torn, neither choice giving me anything to work with. Unless, the thought came to me, I didn't let her know I was awake at all. If she wanted to talk to me, she could wake me up. In that case, I could let her speak first and base my response on her words. And if she didn't, it would've been her choice not to say good-bye.

The doorknob turned and I made my decision. I closed my eyes and kept my breathing even. I heard her walking, then nothing for a minute or two. I risked opening my eyes a sliver. She was still here, standing at the desk and frowning at a piece of paper. As I watched, she wrote a few lines and set down the pen. I quickly closed my eyes and a moment later, I was glad I had. I felt more than heard her coming towards me and stop next to the bed.

The light brush of her lips against my forehead almost made me lose my resolve and then I felt a drip of liquid on my skin. My stomach twisted. She was crying. It took all of my self-control not to jump up and go to her. I hated knowing that I'd been the cause of her tears and the thought of her in pain made my own heart ache.

Dammit!

When I heard the main door close, I opened my eyes and stared at the ceiling. Had this been a bad idea? Should I have walked away at the club? Not gotten on the train? Not suggested we leave together? I'd had a dozen points where I could've walked away and I hadn't used any of them. Who knew how different things would've been if I'd done the smart thing. It seemed like all I did lately was second-guess my decisions.

I sat up. It didn't matter now. I made my choices and, for better or for worse, I had to live with the consequences. Unfortunately, one of those seemed to be a deeper attachment than I'd ever meant to have.

I swung my legs over the edge of the bed, ready to head into the bathroom for a long, hot shower. That's when I saw it. There was a folded piece of paper sitting on the table next to the bed. I didn't want to read it, but I picked it up anyway. It was brief and I read it three times before the words sunk in.

She planned to move on and she wanted me to do the same. She wished me all the best. I wished her the same. I just wished it could've been with me. She was right, and I hated it. We had to move past this. It was the best thing for everyone involved.

She'd go back to her family and her country. Marry whoever her parents had chosen for her. Become a mother and a queen. I'd finish my trip and figure out what I was going to do with the rest of my life. We both might look back on these couple days fondly, but that's all they would be. Memories.

I ran my hand through my hair as I stood. It was time to let go. Time to do as she'd said and move on. Still, a part of me said to go after her, to tell her that we owed it to ourselves to see where this could go. I silenced the voice as I walked into the bathroom.

Shower, then eat. After that, I'd move on with the rest of my life. Our time was up.

Continues in Exotic Desires Vol. II, release May 5th.

Other book series from M. S. Parker

Casual Encounter Box Set

Sinful Desires Box Set

Club Prive Vol. 1 to 5

French Connection (Club Prive) Vol. 1 to 3

Chasing Perfection Vol. 1 to 4

Broken Pleasures

Forbidden Pleasures

His Pleasures

Dark Pleasures

More Pleasures – release April 24th

Pure Pleasures – release May 12th

Exotic Desires series – release April/May 2015

Acknowledgement

First, I would like to thank all of my readers. Without you, my books would not exist. I truly appreciate each and every one of you.

A big "thanks" goes out to all my Facebook fans, street team, beta readers, and advanced reviewers. You are a HUGE part of the success of my series.

I have to thank my PA, Shannon Hunt. Without you my life would be a complete and utter mess. Also a big thank you goes out to my editor Lynette and my wonderful cover designer, Sinisa. You make my ideas and writing look so good.

About The Author

M. S. Parker is a USA Today Bestselling author and the author of the Erotic Romance series, Club Privè and Chasing Perfection.

Living in Southern California, she enjoys sitting by the pool with her laptop writing on her next spicy romance.

Growing up all she wanted to be was a dancer, actor or author. So far only the latter has come true but M. S. Parker hasn't retired her dancing shoes just yet. She is still waiting for the call for her to appear on Dancing With The Stars.

When M. S. isn't writing, she can usually be found reading– oops, scratch that! She is always writing. ☺

Printed in Great Britain
by Amazon

30191202R00112